story by †
SHU

illustrated by †
Shizumayoshinori

The Misfit of Demon King Academy

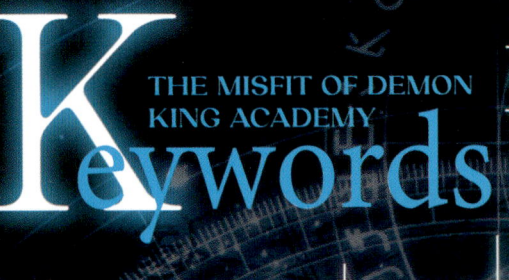

Keywords

THE MISFIT OF DEMON KING ACADEMY

The Mythical Age

The era of war and chaos that occurred two thousand years ago, before Anos's reincarnation. Demons, humans, spirits, and gods lived in a world in constant conflict, but the carnage between demons and humans was particularly brutal.

The Magical Age

The era of peace that followed the Mythical Age. Contrary to its name, magic technology has degraded dramatically since the prior era. Many higher grade spell formulae have been forgotten, with some spells being entirely lost to time.

A greater magic spell that the Demon King of Tyranny activated with the help of the Hero, Goddess of Creation, and Great Spirit. This was the spell that separated the world into its respective species, allowing for the two thousand years of peace since.

Beno Ieven

A school founded with the intention of raising demons of high status to become the next generation of demon lords. However, with the approach of the Demon King's reincarnation, it has also taken on the role of selecting superior demons worthy of becoming a vessel. The building is the same as the former Demon King Castle Delsgade.

Demon King Academy Delsgade

The Seven Demon Elders

The seven demons Anos created from his own blood two thousand years ago, who are now leaders of demonkind. Created and given life through magic rather than natural means, they exist because reincarnation requires a body that has inherited one's blood.

Demons who inherit the blood of the Demon King of Tyranny. Only descendants of the Demon King may enroll at the Demon King Academy. Amongst them are "royal" families who procreate only through intermarriage, who are of higher status than mixed-race demons.

The Demon King's Descendants

The core of one's existence hidden within every living being. Superior magic users can store their memories in their source and reincarnate with knowledge of their past life. When no physical body remains, resurrection is also possible as long as the source is unharmed.

Source

Sasha Necron

Misha's older twin sister, sixteenth in line to the Necron family. Nicknamed the Witch of Destruction, after the Magic Eyes of Destruction in her pupils.

Misha Necron

Sasha's younger twin sister and relation to Ivis Necron, one of the Seven Demon Elders. Despite her family, she's treated as poorly as demons of mixed blood.

"I have no more regrets," she said, looking me in the eyes. "I thought we'd never be able to make up. But there have been two miracles in my lifetime."

"Don't be absurd."

Misha looked at me, puzzled.

"The real miracle is yet to come."

Anos Voldigoad

The reincarnation of the Demon King of Tyranny, who had power enough to challenge humans, spirits, and even gods. Modern magic technology is unable to measure his power and instead brands him a misfit.

story by †
SHU
illustrated by †
Shizumayoshinori

1

Translation by Mana Z.   Edited by Stephanie Buck

MAOH GAKUIN NO FUTEKIGOUSHA Vol.1 ~ SHIJOSAIKYO NO MAO NO SHISO, TENSEISHITE SHISONTACHI NO GAKKO HE KAYOU ~
©Shu 2018
Edited by Dengeki Bunko
First published in Japan in 2018 by KADOKAWA CORPORATION, Tokyo.
English translation rights arranged with KADOKAWA CORPORATION, Tokyo through TUTTLE-MORI AGENCY, Inc., Tokyo.

English translation © 2022 by J-Novel Club LLC

Yen Press
150 West 30th Street, 19th Floor
New York, NY 10001

Visit us at yenpress.com
facebook.com/yenpress ◆ twitter.com/yenpress
yenpress.tumblr.com ◆ instagram.com/yenpress

First JNC Paperback Edition: August 2023

JNC is an imprint of Yen Press, LLC.
The JNC name and logo are trademarks of J-Novel Club LLC.

The publisher is not responsible for websites (or their content) that are not owned by the publisher.

Library of Congress Cataloging-in-Publication Data is available.

ISBN: 978-1-9753-7305-4 (paperback)

10 9 8 7 6 5 4 3 2 1

LSC-C

Printed in the United States of America

The Misfit of Demon King Academy

§ Prologue: Rebirth

The Mythical Age.

There was once a man who destroyed the human nation, burned the forests of the spirits, and even slayed gods. A man feared as the Demon King.

According to history, this man took tyranny to its extremes. Even reason fell before him.

His name was Anos Voldigoad.

"Well? What do you say?"

Perched on his throne with his arms crossed, Demon King Anos spoke. His words carried a power that could leave the average human trembling in fear, but that wasn't a concern for the people currently before him.

The chosen one of the holy sword that could sever fate, Hero Kanon.

The mother of all spirits, Great Spirit Reno.

And the maker of this world, Goddess of Creation Militia.

Four great figures who could sway the destiny of the world, whose names would be passed down for generations to come, had assembled in the Demon Castle Delsgade.

"I hear your proposal," acknowledged Hero Kanon. "The conditions aren't terrible. But you want to make peace now, after all this time?"

"That's right."

"Demon King Anos, how many humans have you killed until now?"

Anos stared at him coldly. "I could ask you the same, Hero Kanon. How many demons have you killed?" he replied.

Human or demon, who had cast the first stone? There was no way of knowing when so much time had passed. Regardless, that knowledge would not alter what had happened.

Perhaps the start had been trivial—one side killed someone from the other. Then, the other side swore revenge. The rest had been mere repetition. A cycle of murder, revenge, retaliation, and death. Hatred had accumulated between the races, endlessly accelerating the chain of tragedy. Humans and demons were alike in that they detested those who were different from themselves.

"Do you really expect me to trust such words after all your savagery?" Kanon asked in place of an answer.

"What else could I have done? If it weren't for fear of the Demon King, you humans would have wiped out demonkind long ago. Under your pretext of justice, you absolve yourselves of all guilt, going so far as to glorify your fallen as heroes."

"Only because of the cruelties that demons commit."

"It was humanity that forced our hand."

"Are you saying demons bear no blame?"

"There's no right or wrong in war." Demon King Anos glared at the hero. "Kanon. Humans seem convinced that defeating me will bring peace to this world, but will that really be the case?"

"Of course."

"No, it will not. You must be aware of it yourself—that such peace would be an illusion. Even if the Demon King were killed, you humans would start a new fire. This war won't end until one side is completely eradicated. No…"

Anos was merely speaking, yet his immense power made every word carry as if it were laced with a compelling magic. Anyone with weak magic resistance would have immediately succumbed to him.

"Even if demons perish, humans will seek a new enemy. They'll wipe out the spirits for their differences; they'll turn on the gods that created them. And once the gods are no more, you humans will turn on each other."

"It's true. Humans do have their faults, but I want to believe in mankind. I want to believe in the kindness of humanity."

Anos chuckled. The brave Hero Kanon was remarkably softhearted. It wasn't as though he were oblivious to the ugliness of human beings— he just had the courage to trust them.

"Well then, Kanon, how about you choose to believe in the Demon King's kindness as well?"

Kanon wasn't able to respond right away. He was probably doubting the offer.

"Like I've said before, I shall divide this world into four realms: the Human Realm, the Demon Realm, the Spirit Realm, and the Divine Realm. These four new worlds will be separated by walls, the gates of which will remain sealed for a thousand years."

A thousand years of isolation should be sufficient for hostility to fade.

"If I convert this life of mine into magic and join forces with the three of you, it'll be possible to activate a spell of such scale."

"You're willing to die for the sake of peace? You, the one known as the Demon King?"

"Your people were the ones to decide on that name. And I shan't die completely—I intend to reincarnate once I find a suitable vessel. Though that isn't likely to happen for another two thousand years."

Kanon fell silent.

After some time, he came to a decision. "Fine... I'll trust you."

Despite being the one who made the proposal, Anos was clearly surprised. He had placed all his sincerity into his explanation. He had even proven that there would be no drawbacks for humans, spirits, or gods. The only remaining issue was the deep-rooted resentment and enmity that had accumulated between them.

That's why he knew it had taken true courage to say that. Anos finally understood why this man was called a hero.

"Thank you."

Kanon seemed surprised by those unexpected words. He smiled faintly. "I never imagined I'd see the day when I'd be thanked by the Demon King."

"And I never thought the day would come when I'd be thanking the Hero."

The two looked each other in the eye. Despite their differences, they both recognized the other's strength and indomitable drive. It was at this moment that their long battle finally paid off.

"Let's begin immediately."

The Demon King rose slowly from his throne and held his hand out before him. In that instant, countless particles of black light began to rise throughout the castle, revealing magic runes that lined the walls, ceilings, and floors. The entirety of Delsgade was a giant three-dimensional magic circle.

"My body will be the gateway."

Anos stepped forward, exposing his defenseless frame.

The Great Spirit was the first to lift her palm at him, followed by the Goddess of Creation. They fired a bright white wave of energy—a near-infinite mass of magic that shone so blindingly, it was like seeing a star up close.

Their purpose was to feed energy through the gate in order to supply the circle, but even the body of the great Demon King could not withstand such power.

Finally, the Hero drew his holy sword.

"What about your rebirth preparations?"

"That's already been taken care of. Now, come."

The violent torrent of magic sparked and cracked like fireworks, bursting loudly in their ears. Unable to endure the activation of a spell that gathered practically all the magic in the world, the castle began to collapse.

Kanon burst into a run, thrusting his holy sword forward. The pure-white blade filled with magic pierced straight through the Demon King's heart.

"Guh..."

Blood dripped from Anos's chest. His mouth became wet with red.

With this, his goal would be fulfilled. He had grown tired of it—the fighting, the futility. He was fed up with it all.

"Kanon, I thank you once more. If you happen to be reborn in two thousand years' time..."

"I shall do so as your friend."

Anos laughed. "Farewell."

Thus, the body of the once great Demon King disappeared in a flash of light.

$$* * *$$

Two thousand years later.

A baby was born to a human family.

"Look, darling... Our baby..." said the woman, Izabella, who held her newborn in delight. Beside her was her husband, Gusta.

"He's adorable. Let's hope he grows into a fine young man," Gusta said, poking the baby's cheek.

"Have you thought of a name for him, my dear?"

"Yes, his name is—" Gusta was about to speak, but a certain small bundle finished the sentence for him.

"Anos. My name is Anos Voldigoad."

Gusta and Izabella's jaws fell open, their eyes bulging from their heads in shock.

"Hmm. Two thousand years passed by in an instant," the baby mumbled to himself; then he looked at the surprised couple. "Oh, forgive me. Is it your first time seeing a reborn child? I know I must have surprised you, but I am, indeed, your child in this era. Take good care of me."

"He…"

"He…"

"He…?" Anos repeated.

"HE SPOKE!" the couple yelled in unison.

Anos made a face. It was only natural for one reincarnated as a baby to speak, wasn't it?

"In fact, it's rather difficult to enunciate in this body. I'm going to grow a bit."

A magic circle appeared around Anos's small form. He suddenly grew at a rapid speed, reaching an age of six or so.

"That should do for now."

With a thump, Anos's feet settled on the floor.

"Wha…ah…oh…"

"Whuh…uh…ah…?"

He looked over at the dumbfounded couple to see them trembling from head to toe.

"He… HE GREW UP!"

Anos pulled another face. It was only natural for one reincarnated as a baby to use Kurst to age a few years, wasn't it?

§ 1. Invitation from Delsgade

One month after reincarnation.

After some casual investigation into the modern world, I found that magic proficiency had declined more than I had expected.

Firstly, it seemed that humans weren't even aware of Syrica, the reincarnation spell. Such practices had been common knowledge back in the Mythical Age, when it hadn't been unusual for even humans with advanced magic to reincarnate. But in the modern era—the Magical Age—there were no known human reincarnators, at least to the general public.

My parents, Gusta and Izabella, were convinced that I was merely an extremely intelligent child. One that could talk from birth and had a knack for magic, that is. Kurst was considered an advanced spell in this era; nevertheless, it was just barely known. Their lack of acknowledgment regarding my reincarnation was inevitable.

More surprising to me, however, was my reincarnation as a human child.

The seeds had first been sown two thousand years ago. I had used magic to create seven subordinates from my blood and commanded them to produce descendants. A perfect reincarnation required a vessel of my own blood.

As predicted, the bloodline of the Demon King Anos had persisted for two thousand years, but I had never expected it to be mixed with the blood of humans.

No, perhaps the occurrence of mixed blood was only natural after a war between races had ended. Deep down, perhaps I, too, had believed that humans and demons could never get along. And yet, in the thousand years it had taken for the walls between the four realms to fall, humans had been isolated from demonkind and in that time had gradually forgotten their woes until such feelings had dissipated in their entirety.

As proof of that, humanity no longer possessed ample knowledge about the demon race. I had tried asking my parents, but they were no more familiar with the subject. They were aware that demonkind existed in a faraway land, but they lacked any further expertise. After all, we lived far from Dilhade, kingdom of the Demon Realm.

"Hm?" I detected a faint wave of magic outside the room.

When I opened the window, a single owl flew inside, dropping a letter into my hands. It was an invitation—to the Demon King Academy Delsgade.

"Demon King Academy...?"

Delsgade was the name of my castle, but I had no recollection of an academy. It had probably been established in the last two thousand years, but what for?

While I was pondering the question, the owl opened its beak.

"Delsgade is an educational institution dedicated to the training of future demon lords. It was created for the sake of the Demon King of Tyranny's descendants—primarily for demon royalty."

The Demon King of Tyranny, huh? That was an old nickname. I had once been called it equally as often as the Demon King Anos, but it seemed the nickname had been more convenient to pass down through the generations.

"Founded by the Demon King of Tyranny, the academy exists to ensure those closely related to him will successfully come to reign over districts of Dilhade as demon lords. You are a descendant of the founder. Thus, I have come to deliver your invitation to Delsgade. The Demon King Academy awaits your enrollment."

A descendant of the founder? I was the founder himself!

The owl had probably found me by following the unique traces of magic that flowed from my blood, but I couldn't really expect a familiar to look any deeper into the abyss. At a glance, this newly born body hosted only the diluted remnants of the founder's blood. But upon closer inspection with Magic Eyes, it would be clear that the blood of the Demon King had merely mutated.

Technically speaking, I was a one-month-old baby. The invitations must have been sent out indiscriminately to anyone who fulfilled their conditions—seemingly, possessing a certain amount of magic along with the founder's blood. Age, after all, was no barrier to demons who could use Kurst.

"This is said to be the year the founder will be reborn."

The date of my return must have been passed down through the generations.

"Many of this year's enrolling student body are so promising, they're being dubbed the Cohort of Chaos. There are high hopes that the reincarnation of the founder is amongst them. In the event of the founder's return, Delsgade will erupt with the jubilation of all demonkind."

I see. In other words, the Demon King Academy existed to find my reincarnated self. In that case, I couldn't leave them waiting. By all means, I wanted to see this promising Cohort of Chaos for myself.

"I accept the invitation."

"The academy eagerly awaits your arrival, descendant of the founder."

The owl flew off.

With that decided, there was no time like the present.

If I was to visit Delsgade, however, my current form would be somewhat inadequate. I used Kurst once more, which enveloped my body with light as it grew to the age of sixteen. A glance in the mirror revealed a black-haired, black-eyed young man. My features were more gentle than I would have liked, but there was enough of a resemblance to my former self.

Well, that was reincarnation for you.

I left my room and headed towards the front door. It was the middle of the night, and mom and dad were asleep, so I shouldn't have any difficulty leaving. Or so I thought as I placed my hand on the door.

"Who's there?!" mom's voice called out from behind me.

Hmm, so she was awake. I hadn't expected that, but surely she wouldn't even recognize me in my new form. At any rate, I turned around to explain myself.

"Anos, dear? Did you grow bigger again?" she asked the instant she saw my face.

"How could you tell?"

"How couldn't I? No matter how much you grow, you'll always be my little Anos."

It was somewhat embarrassing to go from "Demon King" to "little Anos," but I'd had no luck correcting her so far.

"Where are you going so late at night? It's not safe out there."

I may have reincarnated, but that didn't change that I was her son now. Now that I'd been discovered, I couldn't just leave without a word.

"Have you heard of the Demon King Academy, mom?"

She tilted her head in confusion. "I haven't. Is it a school somewhere?"

"Yes, but it's rather far from here. It's in Dilhade."

"What do you need from such a distant school?"

"I've been invited to attend. I'm thinking of enrolling."

"You can't go to a school so far away—it's too dangerous! You're only one month old, Anos!"

Hmm. How troubling. I might have only been born a month ago, but one can't treat a reincarnated man like he's a baby. That said, mom didn't know the first thing about demons, nor did she believe in reincarnation.

"I can't go with you somewhere as far away as Dilhade, Anos. Isn't there a magic academy closer to home?"

"There's nothing for me to learn at a *magic* academy. Besides, I can go alone—there's no need for you to come with me."

"Absolutely not. I told you, you're still one month old. I can't let you live alone at that age. What will you do about money?"

"I can earn it myself."

"How? The world isn't as kind as you think—"

Magic gathered in the palm of my hand, forming a small gold mass.

"What...? No way... This isn't a replica created by magic... It's the real thing!"

Mom was an appraiser by trade, so she specialized in the valuation of precious metals. The moment she saw the gold, she understood how easy it would be for me to make money with such a skill.

"How did you produce this, Anos? Not even the castle sage can use this kind of magic."

Her astonishment was considerable—of course it would be. The castle sage was one of the best magicians in the country. Being unable to use magic of this level would have been unthinkable in the Mythical Age, even for those of the human nation—it would have meant certain death. The modern world had seemingly become a much more peaceful place.

"Making real objects is basic creation magic, mom. Creating fictitious metals such as mythril and orichalcum is elementary. Child's play for the Demon King Anos."

Perhaps that would make her believe in my reincarnation a little.

"I-It doesn't matter if you can use amazing magic—no means no. And my little boy just called himself Anos, didn't he? A mature adult doesn't refer to himself in the third person. Okay?"

Hmm. I hadn't expected that argument...

"What is this Demon King Academy, anyway? What do you study there?"

What was I to do about this? It would be easy to use force, but...

"It's all right, Izabella." Dad joined us from the back of the house. "There's no holding a man back from the path he's decided on."

"But dear, our little Anos is only one month old. And there's no telling what kind of place this Demon King Academy is."

"They say a boy can become a man overnight, right? Anos is one month old now, so he's had thirty times as long. Although I can't say my growth spurts were quite as dramatic."

Indeed. After living with my parents for the past month, there were two things I'd learned: mom was an extreme worrywart, and dad wasn't the sharpest knife in the drawer.

"I understand how you feel, Anos. If it's called the Demon King Academy, then it must be a school that teaches magic to kings. You're talented at magic, so you want to study it properly, right?"

"That's the gist of it. Kind of..."

His deduction wasn't completely incorrect, so I just left it at that.

"Go, Anos," dad said, encouraging me.

"You're sure?"

Dad nodded. "But we're going with you."

...What?

"It's a parent's duty to support their child's ambitions. That said, you're one month old. That's far too young to go off alone."

"You needn't worry about me..."

Dad wagged his finger, tsking at me. "You don't get it, Anos. Listen up. When a child leaves the nest, their parents feel lonely. You've only just been born, so we'll feel that loneliness even more keenly."

Dad was using more complex words than usual. He didn't need to push himself to make his point, though.

"Don't you agree, Izabella?"

"Yes... I never imagined you'd grow up so fast. I'm sorry, Anos. I know you're probably a prodigy blessed by a god, so maybe you feel like I'm just getting in your way, but...won't you let me stay by your side a little longer?"

Even I struggled for words at that.

Before my reincarnation, I didn't even have parents. My mother was dead. I never found out if my father had died or if he'd simply abandoned me. At the very least, I'd never spoken to either parent, which was why I had no particular attachment to them, but...

"If you'd miss me, I guess it can't be helped."

Mom beamed from ear to ear.

"All right, it's decided! We'll get ready to move right away. Don't worry, your good ol' dad's a blacksmith. I can find work anywhere!"

And so, our family moved to Dilhade.

§ 2. Inadequate Descendants

A few days later.

The familiar front gate of my castle stood before me.

The structure had been built as a three-dimensional magic circle, so even after two thousand years, its grand form remained unchanged. At its core was a special magic that allowed it to automatically regenerate, even when its most vital components were destroyed. A substantial part of the castle had collapsed when I had created the walls between the realms, but it was now restored to its former grandeur. The only notable difference was its new title of Demon King Academy.

The many people around me were entering the gate one after another. Presumably, they were also prospective students here to take the entrance exam.

"Do your best, Anos!" mom called, chipper as ever.

Despite me assuring them it was unnecessary, both mom and dad had insisted on seeing me off at the gate when they had learned I'd be taking the entrance exam.

"A-Anos! R-R-Remember to stay c-c-calm!" Dad was stuttering profusely.

"Perhaps you should calm down too, dad."

"R-Right. Sounds like you'll be fine."

"Yup, yup! Our little Anos is already so reliable at one month old. He's sure to pass!"

Of course, none of the other students had come here with their parents. The gazes of those around us bored uncomfortably into me.

"I'll be going now." I turned on my heels and made my way over to the line of demons before the gate.

"Go, go, Anos! Fight, win, Anos!"

Hmm. Perhaps that's a little too much, dad...

So this was what having human parents was like, huh? It wasn't so bad, actually. Just a little embarrassing.

Just then, another embarrassing voice rang out from behind me, sounding alongside dad's.

"Hooray, Misha! You've got this, Misha!"

I glanced over my shoulder to see a rugged man with a beard yelling his heart out. There was some demon blood in him, just as there was in dad, but the scent of human blood was stronger. A human, then.

The man's gaze was fixed on a girl who was walking along with a blank expression, carefully hiding her embarrassment. She had platinum-blonde hair that grew long over her ears with loose waves at the ends. It was hard to tell from the front, but the back was cut much shorter. Her charming features—her blue eyes and button nose—had a hint of child-like innocence left to them.

The black and white robe she wore was embroidered with a design of demonic origin, so perhaps her other parent was a demon.

As I reached the gate, dad's voice grew louder than ever.

"You can do it, Anos! Go, go, Anos!"

The girl who had passed me looked back in curiosity, then followed dad's gaze to me.

"Ah..."

Our eyes met.

"We both have it tough, huh?" I said in greeting.

Her reply was short and quiet. "Yeah..."

Whether shy or simply untalkative, she didn't say another word beyond that. But she didn't seem particularly wary of me either.

"I'm Anos. Anos Voldigoad."

As soon as I said those words, I realized my mistake. It was, after all, the name of the founder. While part of me didn't want to create an unnecessary fuss, another part saw no reason to hide the truth. Well, it would come out eventually. It was only a matter of time.

"I'm Misha. Misha Necron..."

Surprisingly, she didn't comment on my name. I found that a little odd, but whatever. It had been two thousand years. Not everyone had to be interested in the Demon King Anos.

"It's nice to meet you, Misha."

"Yeah..." she said again. All her replies were short and succinct.

Just as we were about to pass through the gate, a man stood in our way. He was dark-skinned with a rock-hard physique, and his white hair was cropped short. He looked to be about twenty years old, and he smirked wickedly as he looked down on us.

"Aww, did mommy and daddy have to hold your hands here? Since when did the Demon King Academy become a playground? Ha!"

Hmm. What kind of opener was that?

The crowd around us began to stir.

"Hey, isn't that..." someone whispered.

"Ah... This is bad. Zepes has set his sights on them. They're not getting away from a jackass like that in one piece..."

It seemed he had quite the reputation.

That aside, the line was veering towards the right. If I remembered correctly, that was where the exhibition arena was located. With that in mind, I supposed the entrance exam would be a practical test.

"Are you good at fighting, Misha?"

"Not really..."

So it wasn't her specialty. Well, that was acceptable for a peaceful world.

We turned right, following the line.

"Hey! You— Hey! I'm speaking to you, jerk!"

The voice was so noisy, I turned around. The man from earlier was glaring at me.

"Hmph. Finally faced this way, huh?"

Good grief, this descendant of mine had no manners. Perhaps a little discipline was in order.

"My bad," I conceded. "Your magic was so weak, I didn't see you."

"Wh…at…?!" The man's eyes widened in fury. "Are you knowingly insulting me, the Demon Duke Zepes Indu?"

"Demon Duke…? Doesn't ring any bells. You're famous?"

Oh, I see. It must be a fresh moniker that had popped up sometime in the last two thousand years.

"You bastard… This is your last chance to apologize."

What a cold voice. Zepes clenched his fist, a hostile look in his eyes. Particles of magic gathered around him to form several magic circles.

One, two, three…five magic circles, huh?

When Zepes opened his fist, a jet-black flame of condensed darkness flickered in his palm.

"Wha…?"

"Ha! Surprised? Fine, let's hear you beg for your life. Get on your knees and kiss my feet if you don't want that girl's face burned to the bone with Gresde, the flame of darkness, consumer of gods! Bwa ha ha ha!"

Wh… What…

What low-level spellcasting! He needed five whole magic circles to use a Gresde of that level?! Even I had been expecting something bigger than a spark after such an arrogant buildup. Not all of my descendants were blessed with great power, it seemed. How pitiful.

"I have no interest in picking on the weak."

I let out a small huff of air. With that, the flame on Zepes's palm went out.

"What the... That can't be! It's impossible!" he yelled in shock. "Y-You bastard... What the hell did you do?!"

"Why the surprise? I blew out the light of your match."

"You're comparing the flame of my Gresde to that of a match?!"

From the outset, the way Zepes and I used our magic was fundamentally different. Zepes had to desperately gather it just to cast a simple spell. If I were to cast the same spell, the power to supply it would come to me naturally.

Being unable to do this in the Mythical Age would have meant certain death... Had complacency in this peaceful world really made magic regress so far? Well, I guess that just meant this was a good era to live in—especially if it allowed demons this weak to talk so big.

"You... Don't think you're getting away with this alive..."

That aside...had this guy still not realized the difference in our strength?

"*Wait.*"

The moment I uttered the word, Zepes stiffened as though his whole body was paralyzed.

"Is something wrong?" I asked him.

"Wha... I...I can't move... What did you...?!"

Ah, I see. The magic permeating my every word had compelled him to obey me. His magic resistance was so pathetic that he could be ordered around with an unintentional verbal jinx.

"Just stand there and repent for a while."

The next instant, Zepes's face crumpled with regret. "What have I done...? How could I speak to a stranger like that? Oh, if only the ground would swallow me... How could I ever apologize for this?" Zepes continued his repentance while he stood as still as a scarecrow.

The bystanders let out a collective gasp.

"Whoa, that guy's something else. Zepes is apologizing to him..."

"Yeah, did you see how he canceled Gresde like it was nothing? He must be pretty skilled at counter magic..."

"I don't even recognize his face. What if he's a dark horse of the Cohort of Chaos...?"

They sure liked to exaggerate. At any rate, I suppressed my voice after that—he should be released after ten minutes or so.

"Sorry to keep you waiting. Shall we go?" I asked Misha, who had been waiting for me to finish.

We walked off together.

"Anos..." she said quietly.

"What is it?"

"Are you strong...?"

I let out a chuckle. "I won't deny it. But that wasn't the matter here."

Misha gave me a puzzled look. "What was the matter?"

"He was just too weak."

With that, we entered the arena where the examination was being held.

§ 3. Practical Test

The line split before the arena. Statues of knights stood in a row nearby, and an owl was perched atop one of them.

"Please line up in groups as written on your invitation," it said.

I looked at my invitation. It had the letter F on it.

"What's yours, Misha?"

"E." She flipped over her own to show me.

At the end of each line were more owls, each holding a scrap of parchment with a coordinating letter written on it. We were probably meant to line up there.

"Then I'll see you once we've enrolled."

"Yeah."

I bid farewell to Misha and lined up in row F. The front of the line was far in the distance, but I could see the proceedings with my Magic Eyes of Farsight. They appeared to be letting people into the waiting room one by one.

Naturally, it would take some time for my turn to come. There were roughly one hundred people in this line alone—a total of seven hundred across all the groups. I know two thousand years had passed, but that was quite a lot of descendants. It appeared there had been no need to worry about my bloodline dying out.

I continued to ponder vacantly while waiting for time to pass.

After a while, I reached the front of the line, then entered the waiting room before me. Inside was yet another owl.

Whose familiar was this, anyway? From what I could see, it bore no trace of magic power. All signs of its master were skillfully hidden. There was at least one person in this era capable of using decent magic, then.

"Welcome to the entrance exam. I shall now explain the particulars of the practical test."

After they'd sent out all those invitations, there would be a test anyway... So admittance into the school was still yet to be determined, huh? Their greater purpose was to locate the reincarnated founder after all.

This was my first time reincarnating. It wasn't that rare to retain one's past memories in doing so, but the demons of this era had no idea how much awareness the Demon King Anos would have of himself. They only possessed the vague knowledge that the reincarnation of the founder would be amongst the students enrolling this year.

The Cohort of Chaos was said to be promising, so they must have already shown enough power to be dubbed as such. That meant it was unlikely they had only been born one month ago like I had.

They perhaps hadn't expected the founder to reincarnate as a baby, but rather within an existing vessel that already possessed great strength. There was also the possibility of returning without any immediate memories or abilities.

True, it would be easy to announce myself and end their search instantaneously, but they'd gone through all this trouble for me. It would only be polite to go along with their plans.

"In the practical test, candidates will duel one another in the arena. Those who defeat five others will undergo a test that measures magic and determines aptitude, before being accepted into Delsgade. Those who are defeated will be declined admission."

Because there was no way the Demon King would lose, right?

The examination also had the potential to determine the founder from their application of magic. It was a somewhat simple test format, but it was sufficient.

"The use of any form of weapon, armor, or magic item is permitted. Do you have any questions?"

"No."

"Then may the founder bless you."

I opened the waiting room door. A dimly lit stone corridor extended outside.

Although it was part of my own castle, the arena had originally been built for exhibition matches. It was my first time using this passage.

After walking for a while, I saw light streaming in from outside. I stepped outside to find myself in a circular arena bordered by a towering wall. The spectator seats were located above the wall and were occupied by the odd demon. They all wore the same uniform so were presumably students of the academy.

"Yo. So we meet again."

On the opposite side of the arena stood a dark-skinned man. It was that Zepes fellow I'd brushed off earlier.

Hmm. It'd be hard to show off my powers as founder against such a weak opponent... What was I to do now?

"Hey, are you even listening, bud?!"

I took one, two, then three silent steps forward when the passageway behind me was suddenly sealed with a magic barrier.

"Oops!" Zepes called smugly. "It seems I've blocked your chance of escape. What, you scared?"

"On the contrary, I'm merely pitying you for cornering yourself. But don't worry, I'm not going to kill you."

Zepes clicked his tongue in disgust.

Hmm. There was no need for that—I was only being considerate. Could it be that he still didn't understand our difference in power? Surely he couldn't be so stupid...

"Just so you know, I'm not a coward like you. Your smug face will be a bawling mess by the time I kill you."

I couldn't help myself—I burst into laughter. "Ha ha haaa! No wait, say that again. Who are you killing? Me?" I glared at Zepes. "*Know your place, fool.*"

Although my words flowed naturally with magic power, Zepes wasn't compelled to follow my order. His newly donned dark-gray armor had activated a circle of magic resistance.

"Heh. I'm not falling for that trick again. This anti-magic armor has the power to ward off any kind of magic."

I see. His dependence on such toys had weakened his resistance to magic. This descendant of mine never ceased to find new ways to disappoint me.

"The use of any form of weapon, armor, or magic item is permitted. Victory will be decided when one side dies or surrenders," the owl's voice echoed from above. "Now, let the practical test begin!"

Immediately, Zepes drew the sword at his hip. The blade burned with a brilliant flame.

"Surprised? The Demon Sword Zephrid has been passed down through the Indu family for generations. Its blade was forged in ancient flame and has the power to increase my power tenfold. You may have a high resistance to magic, but you've no chance in hell of blowing out this flame!"

"Hmm. Is math a weakness of yours?" I asked as he closed the distance between us.

Zepes flew into a rage. "What are you trying to say...?!"

"Ten times zero is still zero, you know."

"Shut your mouth!" Zepes burst into a run. The next moment, he appeared before my eyes, raising his demon sword. "Now die."

Haaah… Oh, I failed to stifle my yawn.

Still, he sure was taking his time. If I were the one holding that sword, I would have swung it a hundred times by now. But it would be immature of me to use my full power playing with a child. I'd do this at his level.

Fancy weapon aside, the skill of its user made it pointless to even dodge.

With a vicious horizontal slash, Zepes swung the flaming Zephrid at my throat. Distracted from my daydream, I looked up…and saw the sword properly for the first time.

Oh! I dodged the swing at the last moment.

"Heh. You're pretty good at dodging."

Phew. That was close. A millimeter closer and the faint anti-magic field that constantly surrounded me would have snapped his sword in two. He'd mentioned the weapon had been passed down through the Indu family for generations. No matter how dull a blade it was, I'd feel bad if I destroyed something so important. But that aside…

"So that's a demon sword?" I inquired.

"That's right. This your first time seeing one? This thing uses proper magic, unlike what you'll have become used to seeing today. An ancient blade infused with power. An artifact of the Mythical Age. This is the Demon Sword Zephrid!"

This was a demon sword…? A twig lying on the floor in the Mythical Age would have held more power. He claimed it was an artifact of that time, but he must have received a fake. Real demon swords had their own will. Their power was so tremendous, they would consume their own wielder. The term "demon sword" had come to be used so frivolously.

"Haaah," I sighed without thinking.

The flame of the demon sword flickered out.

"Wh-Whaaa—?!" Zepes's ugly screech was accompanied by the surprised gasp of the audience.

"I...I can't believe it...! He blew out the flame of Zephrid!"

"But it was said the ancient flame would burn till the end of the world... He didn't even need a magic circle!"

Zepes gritted his teeth. "You... Did you just use sealing magic?!"

"No, I simply blew it out. But with the magic infused in that sword, it's sure to start burning again in a few years."

His expression turned sour. "First compulsion magic, now sealing magic. Your power may be impressive, but your spells are all defensive. Do you really think you can get past anti-magic armor with tricks like that?"

Hmm. That so-called armor looked like it would shatter with a featherlight touch, but would it be too immature of me to say such a thing?

"I wouldn't call doing so much of a feat."

"Heh. So you're scared."

"No, but I have an interesting proposition for you. You and I should never have been placed on the same playing field in the first place."

Zepes glared at me warily.

"So, here's a handicap: I won't take a single step from this spot. I won't use magic circles, and I won't imbue my words or breath with magic. I shall defeat you without moving my arms, legs, hair, eyes—that's right, I won't even blink."

"Ha! At least make your bluffs believable. Or is that an excuse for when you lose? It seems you really don't have any offensive spe—" Blood spewed from Zepes's mouth. "No way... Wha...is this..."

"Did you hear it?"

Badump.

"The sound of my heartbeat."

The sound of my beating heart, filled with magic power, jolted Zepes's entire body. The anti-magic armor he wore was far from a quality item—there were a number of gaps in the magic circle, which my heart-beat passed right through.

"Guh... Aagh..."

Blood spurted from all over Zepes's body as he fell to his knees and then collapsed forward.

"Hmm. This is troubling. If everyone's so weak, I'll end up killing people whenever my pulse quickens."

§ 4. The Common Sense of the Demon King, Two Thousand Years Later

I turned around to walk away when a voice called out from behind me.

"Hold it...right there..." Zepes tried to get up, but his wounds were too severe. With his body uncooperative, he crawled along the ground.

"You'll survive if you receive immediate treatment. I recommend you surrender."

"Ha. That's what I thought, you disgrace of a demon... Calling yourself a descendant of the founder when you can't even finish off your enemies..."

Was he talking about the lineage of the Demon King? I didn't need to call myself a descendant—I *was* the founder.

"If you talk too much, you'll die."

"Kill me."

"I would, but there isn't much value in killing small fry like you."

Now, what was I to do?

"Ha! Can't do it? Go on, just try to make me surrender. I'd rather die than give in!"

If I ordered him to surrender, he'd probably do so immediately...

"I know what you're thinking. You're gonna fall back on your compulsion magic, no? Go ahead—try it. You know you'll never get me to give up, right?! Ha ha ha! Bwa ha ha ha ha— Oof!"

I stepped on Zepes's head, pressing his face against the stone floor. "Good grief, how haughty. You want to bask in such puny superiority so badly? What a miserable fellow."

However, he had said something rather interesting.

"So you think I can't make you surrender without compulsion magic, huh?"

"It… It's true, isn't it? You scum…!"

Despite having his head stepped on, Zepes continued to argue back. He sure was enthusiastic for a petty underling.

"Hmm. An interesting idea. All right, I'm in. If I make you surrender without the use of compulsion magic, I win. If not, you win."

"Ha, you sure you should be talking so big? I'd rather die than surrender!"

With the blink of an eye, I activated Zecht—contract magic. The terms stated that if I couldn't make Zepes surrender without the use of compulsion magic, I would surrender myself.

Zecht was absolute. The caster and those who signed the contract with their magic were bound by it.

Zepes signed without hesitation. "You dumbass… No matter how much pain you inflict, I won't surrender… You're going to regret this! Ha ha ha ha!"

I brought my index finger before his forehead…

"Hah? What—"

…and flicked it.

"—are yooou—?!"

Zepes's entire body splattered across the field.

"Oh… I thought I was holding back enough, but I killed him anyway… I see."

Goodness. At this rate, it'd be my defeat. There was no helping it. I cut the tip of my index finger, letting a single drop of blood drip down.

Ingall.

Zepes's body regenerated; he was resurrected in an unharmed state. I even modified his sword and armor to strengthen it a little.

The audience was dumbfounded.

"Wha... What is that magic?! Zepes was dead!"

"He was brought back from the dead...?! I've never heard of a spell like it!"

What were they so shocked for? The audience was making a lot of fuss over something so trivial as Zepes coming back to life. If one couldn't perform such magic, death would mean actual death.

"Wha... I..." Zepes looked at me with a befuddled expression.

"Well? How did you like dying? Feel like surrendering yet?"

"N-No way... Who would ever surrender to y— Gah...!"

I flicked my finger again, killing him.

"Ha ha, oops. I accidentally killed you again. But it's fine; as long as I use Ingall within three seconds, there's no risk of permanent death. You may know it as...the three-second rule."

A deathly hush fell over the spectator seats.

Hmm. Had I, of all people, failed to land a joke?

The three-second rule had been a surefire quip in the Mythical Age... How could it have fallen flat? Standards of comedy must have changed in the past two thousand years. In fact, upon closer inspection, everyone looked mortally horrified. Was my joke really that terrible? I'd have to hold back on the jokes until I understood the Magical Age better.

"Ah...!" Zepes, having been once more resurrected through Ingall, looked at me with fear.

Now, time to corner him gently. Enough not to cause any trauma, that is.

"You said you'd rather die than surrender, but did you think you'd only die once?"

Zepes didn't reply—he was too busy trembling.

"Now, let me ask you again: do you feel like surrendering yet?"

Despair flashed in Zepes's eyes, but he managed to squeak in a feeble voice, "S-Someone, hel— Aagh...!"

Figuring it would take one more push, I killed him again. Even so, the single drop of blood required for Ingall sure was bothersome.

When Zepes's body regenerated once more, he looked at me in pure terror.

"By the way, there's an intriguing philosophical dispute related to Ingall. If a person is brought back to life, are they the same person that died? Or are they a different person with the same personality, memories, and body? What's your take?"

Zepes's teeth chattered behind his trembling lips. His face was as pale as a sheet. "Y-You bastard... You're insane..."

"Hmm. Not interested in the debate, huh? It was a heavily discussed topic back in my day."

Well, if the standards of comedy had changed so much, I shouldn't be surprised if interests in philosophy differed as well.

"Oh well. I guess I'll try killing you one more time."

"Y-You... You talk about killing so easily..."

Even I chuckled heartily at that one. "What's wrong? That's a rather drastic change of heart. It's not as though you'll die permanently," I said lightly, bringing my hand to Zepes's forehead.

"Wa... Wa... Wait, please..."

"Huh?"

Oh. Oops. My finger slipped, and I killed him again. How careless of me—it seemed I still wasn't used to this new body. He was just about to say something too. Well, I could just hear it after resurrecting him. *Ingall.*

"Y-You jerk! I asked you to wait!"

"Ha ha, sorry. My finger slipped."

"Don't laugh at me, you bastard! Who kills with a slip of a finger?!"

"Oh? Still lively, I see. Let's do one more round, then." I brought my finger to Zepes's forehead once more.

He immediately shrank back, paling further. "W-Wait..."

"What now? There's no room for hesitation in the midst of battle."

"It's…" His expression was filled with humiliation, but his words were clear. "It's my loss. I give up."

Oh? What a letdown.

"Was that all it took to crush your will? How weak of you. Here I was prepared to kill you another ten thousand times." I was joking to express my lack of hostility, but for some reason Zepes trembled even harder.

Voices rose from the spectator seats.

"He just treated Zepes like a kid…"

"That was beyond one-sided… Who is that guy? I've never seen him before…"

§ 5. Royalty

"Zepes Indu has conceded. The victor is Anos Voldigoad."

With the owl's announcement, the magic barrier blocking the exit vanished.

But something was strange—I'd been called Anos just now, yet the audience had shown no reaction. Could there be so many Demon King impersonators out there that they didn't care to respond? Being too famous sure had its downsides. That said, I could always prove I was the real deal with my abilities.

"That was a fine battle." I extended a hand to Zepes, praising his valiant effort.

He flinched back in fear. "Y-You, bastard! I'll remember this!"

After spitting out the words of a cliché villain, he scurried away.

Hmm. There was no need to hold grudges—the match was over. What was he so angry about? Sure, he may have failed the entrance exam because of me, but it wasn't as though I'd taken his life. He could just try again next time. In fact, he had fought with me and left with all his limbs intact. Any demon of the Mythical Age would've been moved to tears.

"The next duel will commence after a ten-minute intermission."

"No need."

This kind of duel couldn't even be considered a warmup. If I had to take a ten-minute break each time, I'd end up bored to death. And there were still four people to go! I could only pray they weren't as weak as my first opponent.

"At the request of Anos Voldigoad, the intermission will be abridged."

Just then, I saw a torrent of magic surging from the corridor Zepes had fled down.

"Gyaaaaah!" someone screamed.

A long-haired demon appeared at the entrance. The demon's brows were knitted together in a volatile expression. In his hand, he clutched Zepes's neck.

"I…I'm sorry, brother…" Zepes whimpered. "Please forgive me. Next time I'll—"

"Have you no shame?" With a squeeze, the long-haired demon crushed Zepes's throat, where particles of magic began to gather. With a crackle of black lightning, his whole body was set alight.

"Gyaaaaaaaaaah!"

In an instant, Zepes was burned to a crisp. The long-haired demon tossed him aside and walked towards me.

"Thanks for looking after my little brother."

I see. This was Zepes's brother, huh? He seemed stronger than his younger sibling, but I can't say he left a favorable impression.

"It would have been much nicer if those words were said to avenge your brother, but alas."

"He has disgraced our bloodline for being bested by a mongrel. My assistance in his atonement was an act of mercy."

By "mongrel," did he mean me? I don't like to pick fault with every little thing, but if I were a mongrel, then he'd be a descendant of a mongrel… Was he okay with that? It was as comical as using "your mother" insults in a fight between siblings.

"Brothers are meant to stand by one another, are they not?"

"How naive. Power defines demon royalty."

Good grief. Who was the naive one here? There was no point killing Zepes simply because he was weak. Even the weak had their uses. In the Mythical Age, reducing one's allies for no reason was the kind of folly that led to one's downfall.

"It seems you have a mistaken understanding of power."

"What drivel. I should have expected as much from someone who plays around with greater magic like Ingall instead of killing and being done with it."

The man spoke as though he'd been watching, so I turned to look at the spectator stands in curiosity.

Ah, so he'd been watching from over there. There were demons in the third row who weren't in the school uniform—most likely fellow examinees. They must be spying on their opponents.

But something didn't add up. After I'd lined up in group F, I had been immediately brought to the arena to commence the practical test. There'd been no opportunity to go to the stands and watch others.

"It seems you're unaware. We, the pure-blooded demon royalty, have the privilege of choosing our opponents. Don't expect we'd be treated the same as mixed breeds that just happen to have inherited a drop of the founder's blood."

Hmm. So the letter written on the invitation indicated the purity of my blood. I don't know who'd come up with that one, but it was laughable. Blood purity was unrelated to the amount of power one inherited. If it were that simple, anyone could have killed my vessel before I'd reincarnated.

Anyway, there was no basis for arguing that pureblood demons were strong, while mixed-blood demons were weak. A single drop of the Demon King's blood was enough. Honestly, I was dumbfounded that no one had realized this.

The long-haired demon acknowledged my silence. "I see you understand your position now."

"Ah, actually, no. I was just contemplating how absurd you are."

A vein at the man's temple twitched. "Absurd, you say...?"

"Think about it. The Demon King was chosen because of their strength. Blood? Status? What does any of that matter? Don't make me laugh," I sneered.

The demon's face twisted into a frown. He may have felt proud of his lineage, but it was meaningless pride.

"I don't particularly care if you create a privileged class—there are people who do so in every era. But the Demon King is one who subverts all laws and politics with power alone. To think his descendants are now the privileged ones..."

Seemingly offended by my mocking tone, the long-haired demon glared at me. His gaze was filled with hostility. "You belittle the founder's great achievements because of your prejudice against royalty! I, the Demon Duke Leorg Indu, will personally execute you."

"How does talking about myself belittle my own achievements?"

"What...?"

"Fool. I'm saying I'm the founder."

Leorg glared at me with a look of pure hatred. "You... Do you know what you're saying?"

"What? That I'm me?"

Unable to hold himself back any longer, Leorg snapped. "You dare to claim the name of the founder?! Such disrespect demands death!"

"Forgive me, but I'm not following. You really thought the reincarnated Demon King would be too stupid to recognize himself?"

"Shut your mouth! Doubting the words of the Seven Demon Elders is a grave sin!"

Hmm. Seven Demon Elders? It was another term new to me, but I'd have to look into it later.

"What you're saying is completely unfounded, but so be it. A Demon King doesn't prove himself with words."

"You...! You dare make light of our Elders?!"

That hadn't been my intention… What an annoying guy.

"Just come at me already. I'll prove to you that I'm the founder."

I expected him to leap at my taunt, but he instead looked towards the spectator seats. "Show this guy what happens to those who criticize royalty," Leorg ordered.

Three demons jumped down into the arena.

"Hmm. Is this okay? We're in the middle of an entrance exam."

Leorg answered smugly. "What are you afraid of? This is part of the test. It would be troublesome to duel one by one, so we're saving you that trouble. Besides, the founder would be able to handle this much."

The owl flying above us was probably acting as referee, but it didn't make any protests. I see. So this was another privilege of theirs. If a royal lacked the power to pass alone, they could resort to methods like this.

"Fine. But four of you?"

"It's too late to change your mind. Reflect on your actions and die."

"What are you misunderstanding now? I'm saying there's too few of you."

Leorg's expression darkened. "What…?"

"Four nobodies aren't enough to prove I'm the founder. Go on and call all of your followers down here."

"You…"

Even without Leorg's command, the demons watching in the stands came rushing down to the arena. These must be members of the so-called royalty—each and every one of them glared at me with discontent. There were roughly eighty in total.

"If you hadn't opened your mouth, you wouldn't have dug your own grave."

"I could say the same to you. Now there'll be eighty needless sacrifices for those graves."

Leorg frowned, but immediately seemed to rethink himself and grinned. "You may be an insolent imposter of the founder, but it would be dishonorable of demon royalty to one-sidedly beat you to death. Ten seconds. We'll give you a ten-second head start. Use that time to prepare whatever powerful magic you wish."

"Oh? I see you're feeling confident with more allies on your side. Pathetic."

Just moments ago, the man had been throwing a tantrum at every statement, but he was all smiles now that his buddies had joined him.

"Do you really have the leisure to chat? Ten seconds is almost up."

Leorg's triumphant words made me laugh in spite of myself.

"What's so funny? Have you lost your mind to fear?"

"You still don't see it? Look with your *Eyes*."

Magic Eyes gave their user the ability to see magic power. At my warning, Leorg finally put his Eyes to work, using his own magic to detect the flow around him. Then, he gasped. He must have noticed how his magic was on the verge of rebelling. The demons surrounding me cried out as well.

"Wh-What is this?! My magic power... It's acting by itself!"

"Impossible... There was no sign of a magic circle. How...? Stop it!"

"He... He was up against eighty of us royals at once... Just how?!"

"What did you do? What's going on?!"

Good grief, how careless could one be?

"Hey, you might want to get your magic under control already. Otherwise..."

The demons surrounding me paled, furiously attempting to regain control over their magic power. But it wasn't enough.

"...you'll die."

The next moment, an earsplitting noise erupted through the arena as eighty demons exploded like fireworks.

§ 6. Forbidden Magic: Origin Magic

The explosion settled, revealing a splay of bodies that spanned the width of the arena.

Still, not a single one of them was dead. It was extremely shameful to see my descendants on the brink of death after I'd gone out of my way to warn them, but at least they had all survived.

"You bastard… What did you do?"

Leorg staggered to his feet. His right arm was stained red, the injury grave enough to render the limb useless for the rest of his life. But aside from that one limb, he was unscathed. Leorg had sent all his magic power into his right arm before it had exploded.

"Oh, that was just a little intimidation tactic. Your sources are trembling in fear of me," I responded.

"Nonsense!"

It was the truth, but Leorg didn't seem inclined to believe it. After all, magic is born from each individual's source. These sources reside within our bodies, beyond our souls, beyond our spirits—deep within the abyss. It's what makes us who we are. When sources of different classes face each other, fear of the greater source can make one's magic go berserk.

The Misfit of Demon King Academy, Vol. 1

"Well, whatever. Are you ready to acknowledge me as the founder?"

Leorg glared at me with contempt. Should I be commending his ability to remain undaunted even now...or should I be admonishing him for being so blind to his opponent's power?

"Never."

"Is that so? But surely you see that I'm closer to the founder than you."

"Sealing magic, compulsion magic, healing magic, and an unknown spell that causes magic power to rebel. There's no way anyone can use so many different types of high-level magic. You're using a special item."

Laughter bubbled up from within me. "Good grief, and now it's magic items? I know you're adamant not to accept my abilities, but your arguments are laughable."

"There's no other way a hybrid could wield that kind of power!"

How had people become so obsessed with lineage? There had been no such way of thinking two thousand years ago.

"As a member of the royal line, I cannot allow myself to fall behind a mere mongrel. Even at the risk of death, I shall never accept defeat!"

Leorg thrust his lifeless arm before him. A magic circle appeared in his palm.

Was that...?

"Very well," he continued. "I shall prove to you the difference between us. This is origin magic, usable only by royalty!"

Sure enough, it was origin magic. I could identify the spell he was casting from the magic circle, but he seemed so pleased with himself, I refrained from raining on his parade.

"Magic power exceeding regulated standards has been detected," the owl announced from above. "The magic barrier and anti-magic field surrounding the stands cannot withstand such magic; casualties amongst the audience are expected. Spectators are requested to evacuate with immediate effect."

Screams erupted from the stands.

"Oh no! Lord Leorg is using *that* spell!"

"Everybody, run! The anti-magic won't hold!"

"Rescue anyone who's unconscious! If they're left here, they'll die!"

The demons in the audience retrieved the eighty fallen royals and fled.

Leorg grinned. "You'll regret your stupidity. Origin magic is a forbidden art. As the caster, I put even my own life at risk."

Black lightning crackled around Leorg's hand. The sparks multiplied until he was covered in a meter-thick dome, then exploded outwards until half the arena was enveloped in the myriad of bolts. The anti-magic field around the stands was hit by the aftermath of magic and let off a barrage of sparks.

"Do you see now?" Leorg said grandly, raising his lightning-clad arm to the sky. "This is true magic—magic that could never be imitated by the likes of a hybrid!"

Then, he swung it down towards me.

"Origin Magic: Jirasd!"

The black lightning expanded several hundred times in size, twisting into a typhoon and blowing apart everything in the arena. Shards of debris rained down from above.

Gradually, the dust cloud cleared, and Leorg emerged from the haze. He had exhausted nearly all of his magic but had somehow managed to survive. Then he saw me.

"Wha—?!" he exclaimed in disbelief. "How did you take a direct hit from Jirasd...and walk away unharmed?!"

His spell had been reasonably powerful, but he'd made one fatal mistake.

"Ancient entities gain magic power in relation to their age. Origin magic is that which borrows from the tremendous power of an ancient origin."

"Th-That's meant to be a secret!" Leorg stammered, flabbergasted. "Where did you...?"

Secret? I was the one who'd developed origin magic. Of course I'd know about it.

"The standard approach to using origin magic is to borrow from the most ancient, most powerful existence possible. However, the older the existence is, the more ambiguous it becomes, making it hard to control the power being borrowed. One often ends up with more power than they can handle."

In short, in order to use origin magic, one must be aware of whose power they call upon. The older the being, the more information lost to time or passed down incorrectly, creating discrepancies with the spell's original existence.

Because of this, it was standard to borrow from an old but proven origin, for example, someone from folklore or legend. Drawing from an ancestor of the same bloodline also increased the chance of success.

The magic Leorg had borrowed for Jirasd was from such an ancestor. An ancestor from two thousand years ago, who had strength enough to slay gods: the Demon King of Tyranny, Anos Voldigoad. In other words, me. Indeed, there was no origin more suitable in this era. However...

"Unfortunately for you, origin magic has no effect on that which it draws power from. Weren't you aware?"

"You still claim to be the founder? This damn hybrid..." cursed Leorg despite his confusion.

I wondered how I should handle the situation. Leorg wasn't as pathetic as Zepes, but he was still rather weak. To me, there wasn't that much difference between them, but Leorg deserved some recognition for casting origin magic at the risk of his life. Perhaps it was time for me to teach him a lesson in magic warfare. As the benevolent founder, it was my duty to look after even the puniest of budding demons.

"You're far from experienced, but I'll commend you for risking your life. Out of respect for your resolve, I'll give you a chance," I said, walking to a particular spot in the arena.

"A chance...?"

"That's right. Just like this."

I stopped and drew a magic circle over Zepes's carbonized form. Then, I reached down and dragged the demon's body from the center. But this time, unlike with Ingall, his flesh was rotten.

"This power... What's with this sinister magic?!"

"Oh, is this your first time seeing it? This is Igrum. Simply put, a spell that resurrects the dead as zombies."

"That's absurd... The corpse is moving as though it's alive! How could you use such a spell...? You're a monster!"

"What? It's not that big of a deal. The spell is simple."

The newly revived Zepes, resurrected as a moving corpse, began his sluggish walk towards Leorg. Darkness swirled in his eyes, drool dripping from his gaping jaw.

"Graaaaaah! It hurts... It hurts, it hurts, it hurts! Brother...why did you kill me? Why did you kill me...? Why?!"

"G-Go away... Begone, you dead bastard! Shoo!" Leorg unleashed Demond at his brother without a moment's hesitation.

"Shut up!" Zepes shrieked.

The black lightning that rushed for Zepes was engulfed in a black flame and instantly consumed. It had been overwhelmed by Gresde.

"Wha—? How did Zepes's feeble Gresde negate my Demond?!"

"That's all thanks to Igrum. Those who have been resurrected gain immense magic power. In exchange, their bodies burn with hatred for their killers, and the pain of their wounds torment them for eternity."

Leorg furrowed his brow. "So you want him to kill me?"

For someone with so much pride, being bested by one's little brother was the ultimate humiliation. He seemed to believe I had used Igrum to make a fool of him.

"Sorry, but I have better taste than that. I told you this was your chance."

"What part of this is a chance?"

"You have a mistaken understanding of power. Zepes, whom you killed with the conception that he was inadequate, has now returned as a zombie stronger than yourself. You must first stop thinking of your brother as deadweight."

Leorg cautiously maintained his distance from Zepes. "Say I stopped thinking of him that way. What then?!" he called.

"Do I have to spell it out for you? Acknowledge your brother, then join forces and face me together."

"What...?!"

It seemed he hadn't expected that response. From what I could tell, Leorg had never combined forces with his little brother in his life, so the thought hadn't even occurred to him. That was why he'd viewed his zombified brother as an enemy.

"Stop spouting nonsense! You just said this zombie burns with hatred for me *and* that he's tormented by never-ending pain! As if someone like that could be remotely sane enough!"

"That's right. It's the suffering of an infernal eternity. Death would be preferable..." I paused before uttering the truth that Leorg was yet to realize. "Even so, brothers are meant to get along."

"Wha—?!"

"Now, show me your brotherly bond. Join forces and come at me as one."

"You can't be serious. Wouldn't it be more merciful to kill him instead?"

"That would be taking the easy way out. Have more faith. Believe in the bonds of brotherhood. There must be moments you spent together without taking heed of your position."

Leorg grimaced, groaning.

Hmm. Perhaps such moments had not existed for them.

"I hate you... Hate... Kill... I'll kill you...!" Zepes murmured deliriously, summoning jet-black flames in his hands. The Gresde in his palms burned as fiercely as his resentment. Leorg would have no chance were he to take a single hit. "Graaah... Ah, it hurts, it hurts, it hurts! I'll kill you... I'll kill you! Aaaaah!"

"Now, what will you do? Your only option is to make up."

Backed into a corner, Leorg would have no choice but to reignite his brotherly bond.

"Unfortunately, I've never thought of him as my brother."

"Cease your whining! Now, if any, is the time to begin getting along. Dispel the hatred between you with all your might. Call your brother's name. Reach out and connect your heart with his. If you fail to reform your bond, you'll die!"

"GRAAAAAH! DIE!"

Zepes's Gresde, formed into a giant fireball, was on the verge of being unleashed at Leorg.

I, however, knew just how powerful the bond between brothers could be. I'd witnessed it myself in the Mythical Age—the sight of a zombified demon protecting his brothers. Sure, demons may have weakened over the generations. Magic had declined, leaving only the most basic of spells behind. But the bond between brothers remained unchanged.

"Call his name!"

At that moment, Leorg found his resolution. "Aaaaagh! Z-Zepes!"

The dark fireball flew straight at him, instantly swallowing the long-haired demon in obsidian flames.

"GRAAAAAAAAAH!" came one final scream as Leorg was reduced to charcoal.

"Hmph."

So this was what brotherly bonds had been reduced to in this era.

§ 7. Aptitude Test

"The practical test has now concluded," the owl's voice echoed overhead. "Candidate Anos Voldigoad may proceed to the Great Mirror Chamber for the next stage."

The Great Mirror Chamber was right beside the arena. Once the barrier blocking the exit had been lifted, I headed for the passageway from which I had originally come.

"Graaah... Waaait... It hurts... I'll kill you... Kill youuu...!"

"Oh dear, I nearly forgot." I turned to look back at the still-zombified Zepes. He was far too pitiful to be left as he was.

One Ingall later and the rotten flesh was back to normal. While I was at it, I resurrected Leorg.

"First you die when you're killed, then you lose your minds over a little zombie resurrection. What troublesome guys."

Both Leorg and Zepes glared in protest but uttered no objections. They must have found themselves speechless before my perfect reasoning.

"See you around. I'll be happy to play with you again when you're stronger," I offered, departing the arena.

"No thanks, you monster..." one of them murmured behind me.

Following the owl's instruction, I made my way to the Great Mirror

Chamber, a room filled with several Great Mirrors. There were many demons already waiting inside—around a hundred or so. They must all be examinees that had passed the practical test.

Amongst them was a familiar face.

"Misha."

Long, platinum-blonde hair swished as she turned to face me.

"You said you weren't any good at fighting, but you made it through the practical."

"I got lucky," Misha replied. She said that, but it took more than just luck to defeat five others. Perhaps Misha was more capable than Zepes and Leorg combined.

"What happens now?" I asked. The itinerary had been mentioned earlier, but I hadn't been interested enough to remember it.

"Passing the practical test secures your admission. All that's left are the magic power and aptitude assessments."

"So everyone here will be our classmates." I cast my eyes around the room, but the atmosphere was somewhat odd. Not a single demon would meet my gaze. In fact, the moment I made eye contact with anyone, they would look away in fear.

"Hmm. Rather shy, aren't they?"

"I don't think that's it..."

"But they won't even look me in the eye."

"They're afraid of your magic."

"Meaning?"

"Igrum."

Ah, that made sense.

"If you know as much, were you also watching from the stands?"

Misha shook her head, expressionless. "Successful candidates are allowed to watch the matches," she said, pointing at the mirror before us.

So that was it. The mirrors in this room were enchanted with far-sight magic that allowed the user to see anywhere within Delsgade. Misha had been watching my test in the mirror.

"I can't comprehend why they would fear Igrum, though. It's not even that bad of a spell..."

Misha stared blankly at me.

"...is it?"

She gave me a silent nod.

"For reference, how bad are we talking?"

Misha paused to think. "It's vile and atrocious."

"Ha ha! Don't be silly. Of all the spells in my repertoire, Igrum is one of the most wholesome, you know?" I said brightly.

She looked at me for a moment, giving it a second thought, then mumbled quietly, "I take it back."

"Of course. As you should."

"It's not the spell that's vile and atrocious. It's you."

"I was just kidding!" I declared, immediately correcting myself. I'd rather tell a few white lies than let my name be sullied with adjectives like those. Anyway, I had only just reincarnated—I had yet to fully understand the values of this age.

"That's a relief."

"You're not afraid of me, huh?"

"There's no reason to be."

That was a rather unexpected line.

"Looks can be deceiving. You have more guts than I thought."

"I'm just normal."

Indeed, it was hard to imagine this detached girl being afraid of anything. She seemed very self-assured—though others might describe her as absentminded.

As I was considering such things, an owl flew overhead.

"The magic power assessment will now commence. Please line up before the power crystal. Once the measurement has been taken, please move to the next room for the aptitude test."

Power crystal? Yet again, this was a term with which I was unfamiliar. There were no items in the Mythical Age that could measure magic power. It seemed that not everything had degenerated in this era.

"So where is this power crystal?"

"Over here." Misha started walking, so I followed her.

The other examinees seemed to know where they were going and had formed several lines by themselves. There were multiple power crystals available to take measurements at the same time.

I observed the measurements taking place. The power crystals were large purple crystals paired with mirrors. Magic power was detected by touching the crystal, and the result was displayed as a numeral on the mirror. The owl in front of the mirrors was reading each number aloud.

"126, 218, 98, 145…"

Measurements of magic power… Power had once been measured by intuition alone. This really was a convenient era to live in.

The assessment only took a few seconds to complete. The line shrank rapidly, and Misha was up next.

"Do your best."

"That won't change anything…"

Fair point. Trying hard couldn't increase one's power.

"Well, good luck, then."

Misha stared at me expressionlessly. "Yeah," she then said, and touched the power crystal.

After a few seconds, the result showed up in the mirror.

"100,246."

Impressive. Until now, the numbers had only reached triple digits, so reaching six was something else. Misha was more talented than I'd thought.

"That's pretty impressive, Misha."

At my compliment, she ducked her head in faint embarrassment. "Are you more impressive, Anos?"

"I am."

Having said that, I touched the power crystal. It was my first time getting my power measured—how large could the number be? Maybe it would break the nine digit mark. If it did, the dull idiots of this generation would have no choice but to recognize me as the founder.

"Zero," the owl read as the crystal shattered into pieces. "Measurement complete. Please proceed to the aptitude test."

Hmm. It didn't seem the slightest bit concerned about the destroyed power crystal.

"I'm fairly certain zero should be impossible," I protested.

"Measurement complete. Please proceed to the aptitude test," repeated the owl.

Zero would mean I couldn't use magic. It was fairly simple logic, but the owl wouldn't hear a word of it. What a useless familiar.

"Familiars can only obey their orders," Misha commented.

"So it seems."

Misha stared at me.

"What's wrong?"

"I've never seen that before..."

"Seen what?"

"Magic power strong enough to break the crystal."

Ah, I see.

Upon analyzing a shattered fragment of the crystal with my Magic Eyes, I discovered that it expanded in reaction to contact with external magic. The volume of expansion was then measured and converted into a number.

However, when that external power surpassed a certain level, the crystal would be unable to expand in response and would instead shatter. I had hoped for a useful invention from this era, but this was far too inadequate to measure my power.

"I would have preferred an 'immeasurable' result over 'zero,' though."

"They can't do that."

"Why not?"

"Power crystals can't break."

"That's been disproven."

Misha closed her mouth for a moment, then said plainly, "You're the exception."

"You can see the truth, can't you?"

"My Magic Eyes are good. Better than anyone else's."

So no one else would be able to see that the power crystal had shattered from exceeding the power limit, huh?

That aside, this school sure liked to leave its entrance exam up to familiars. Brainless birds that could only do as they were ordered couldn't handle unexpected circumstances like the crystal breaking. At best, it could only prepare a new one.

And so, my magic power was deemed unrelated to the destruction of the power crystal.

"The people who can see will know, but most won't be able to," Misha told me.

Good grief. I hoped the school would have more capable people around, but they certainly hadn't been prepared for someone powerful enough to break the crystals—even with the knowledge of the Demon King's return. But from how Misha had described it, the crystals were thought to be absolutely unbreakable.

And all this because the Magic Eyes of this era were so feeble. If one looked carefully into the abyss, it was evident that the crystal would be destroyed by coming into contact with magic that exceeded its limit. Or had they assumed it impossible for even the Demon King Anos to possess such extraordinary power? If so, they'd really underestimated me.

However, it would be immature of me to fuss over a number. It wasn't as though my power had declined or anything.

"Well, it's enough for me as long as you understand," I told Misha.

"Really?"

"Yeah. Thanks."

After another blank look, Misha replied, "You're welcome."

"So, is it that room next?"

She nodded.

As we stepped into the room where the aptitude test was being held, an owl on one of the statues broke the silence. "Step inside the magic circle to begin the test."

A number of magic circles had been drawn across the floor, some occupied by students already taking the test.

"Bye..."

"See you later."

Misha walked towards an unoccupied magic circle, so I went to find one of my own and stood inside it. Then a voice echoed in my head.

"The aptitude test evaluates your mental processes against the standard of the Demon King of Tyranny and reviews your general knowledge of the founder. Your answers will be read from your mind, so cheating is impossible."

They'd read our thoughts using Leaks, huh? It was very amateurish of them to assume the mind couldn't lie—it wasn't even that difficult to do so. That being said, I had no need to cheat.

"Here is your first question: the founding ancestor's true name instills fear too great for it to be uttered aloud. What is that name?"

That wasn't even worth thinking about. The answer was Anos Voldigoad.

"In the Mythical Age, the founder used Jio Graze to devastate Dilhade. The event reduced Dilhade to ashes, and many demons lost their lives. Explain why the founder would perform such a violent act."

Oh, that brought back memories. There was a simple reason I had incinerated Dilhade with Jio Graze: I had been half asleep.

Back then, I had been in the midst of a long battle against Hero Kanon. I'd had to keep my guard up at every moment in preparation for attack. Whether I was asleep or awake, my thoughts had been filled with him. Thanks to that, when Kanon showed up in my dream, I had accidentally let my magic explode.

Nonetheless, there was something slightly wrong with this question. It was true that I'd razed Dilhade to the ground, but not a single demon had been killed in the process. I might have been half asleep, but I had managed to control my magic at the last moment and scorched the city with just the right amount of force to avoid unnecessary casualties. Anyone who couldn't do that much was unworthy of calling themselves Demon King.

"The founder's creed was to kill all who defied him. Explain why this is the proper mentality of a Demon King."

A trick question. I had never uttered such nonsense in my life. If there was no need to kill someone, then I wouldn't—that was my way of doing things. But times were times, and killing had often been the only way to save others. That was all there was to it.

"Suppose there was a powerful daughter with poor Demon King aptitude and a weak son with excellent Demon King aptitude. A god curses both of them to die, but there is only one Holy Grail to save them. Explain who the founder would choose to save."

Hmm. Another absurd question. The answer was simple.

"The next question is…"

Like that, the aptitude test continued. All the questions were related to me, so I was able to answer every one without the slightest hint of hesitation.

Roughly thirty minutes later, the aptitude test ended, and I left the Great Mirror Chamber, ignoring the words of an owl explaining the admission process.

I found Misha standing outside. She wasn't doing anything, just staring blankly into space.

"What are you doing?" I called out.

She looked my way, wearing the same blank expression. "Waiting…"

"For me?"

Misha nodded. "You said you'd see me later."

Come to think of it, I had said that.

"Sorry. I didn't realize the aptitude test was the last thing for the day."

"Yeah."

Still, I couldn't just ditch her after she'd waited for me. That would be too inconsiderate.

"Then, to celebrate our admission, do you want to hang out?"

Misha tilted her head. "Celebrate...with me?"

"Yes."

"Are you sure?"

"I'm the one inviting you."

Misha hung her head in silent thought.

"It's fine if you're busy."

"I'll go..."

"All right. How about we head to my house? Mom's probably got a feast waiting."

She nodded.

"Right, then. Grab on to me." I offered Misha my hand, and she placed hers lightly on top.

"Like this?"

"You'll be left behind like that."

"I can use Fless," she said.

Magic that allowed one to fly in the air. It was fairly useful, but there was a much better spell for traveling.

"It's fine, just hold on tight."

"Okay." Misha squeezed my hand as she was told. A magic circle appeared on the ground, and the scenery before us turned white.

The next moment, a familiar sign appeared before us: "Wind of the Sun." The wooden building housed a blacksmith's and appraisal shop, with a second floor that served as a residential dwelling.

"We're here. This is my house," I said.

Misha remained frozen, staring at the shop sign. There was no change in her expression, but I could tell she was surprised for some reason.

"What spell…?"

"That was Gatom. A spell that connects two spaces for instantaneous movement."

Misha closed her mouth abruptly. After a pause, she mumbled to herself, "Lost magic…"

Hmm. I wasn't quite following, so I asked her what she meant.

"Magic that no one can use anymore," she replied. "Many spells were lost to the Mythical Age."

I see. Proficiency in magic had regressed in these last two thousand years, so while many spells were still known, no one possessed the ability to cast them anymore. That said, Gatom was a spell I had developed myself, so there hadn't been many people who could use it in the Mythical Age either.

"Are you a genius…?"

I couldn't help but burst into laughter.

"I'm being serious…"

"Ah, sorry. I'm not used to being called a genius for something so trivial."

I wouldn't deny that I was a genius, but I'd prefer not to be called one over such simple magic.

"Who are you, Anos?"

"The founding ancestor—the Demon King."

Misha widened her eyes in surprise—the first emotion she'd shown that day.

"The reincarnated…?"

"Do you believe me?"

She thought for a long moment, then asked, "Do you have proof?"

Alas, that was the part everyone wanted.

"I am the proof. My magic power, that is. That said, the Magic Eyes of this generation are too weak to peer into the abyss of my power."

To analyze, to study, to discover the truth... There were many ways of describing it, but the most widely used and all-inclusive phrase was to "look into the abyss." To look into the abyss of magic was to understand its truth and embody it, but to look into the abyss of one's power was what it meant to understand the true value of another.

With a troubled look, Misha fell silent.

The Demon King had originally been proven by strength, but perhaps in this era—that only cared about superficial things like status and the purity of one's bloodline—my way of thinking was a little outdated.

"Your power is endless. Even I can't see its limits."

If Misha couldn't see it, it was unlikely anyone else would. There was no point in troubling her any further.

"You'll find out soon enough. Shall we go?"

"Yeah..."

And I opened the front door.

§ 8. Admission Party

The doorbell clanged as I pulled open the door.

"Welcome, how can I help you— Oh, Anos! You're back!" Mom left her spot behind the counter and hurried over to me. Dad was probably making something in the workshop out back.

"So...how did it go?" she asked nervously.

"I passed."

Mom beamed in relief and wrapped me in a tight hug. "Congratulations, Anos! You did it! My little Anos is so talented, passing an entrance exam at one month old! You're such a clever boy. We're having a feast tonight!"

Goodness. It wasn't like she was the one who'd passed. Was there really a need for such delight? Perhaps this was what it meant to be a parent. I, for one, couldn't comprehend it. Saying that...well, it wasn't a bad feeling.

"What would you like to eat, Anos, dear?"

"Mushroom gratin would be nice."

After two thousand years, it was still my favorite food. My retainers had often urged me to eat something a little more sophisticated and worthy of the Demon King, but I couldn't help liking what I liked. Anyhow, when I'd asked them what a Demon King should eat instead, they would give me the same ridiculous answer: "humans." How could I possibly eat a human? Fools!

They had prattled on about how the image of the Demon King would be ruined by eating gratin, but that was absurd. One with the title of Demon King had enough power to do as they pleased. I could choose to eat what I wanted, when I wanted. And I wanted to eat mushroom gratin.

"He he, all right. You sure love mushroom gratin, don't you? I knew you'd say that, so I already prepared all the ingredients!"

As expected of the Demon King's mother. She was better than all my old retainers combined.

"By the way, mom. We have a guest today."

"Oh? A visitor? Who is it?"

I turned around to introduce Misha, who was hiding behind my back. "This is Misha Necron. I met her at the academy today."

Misha took a step forward. "Nice to meet you," she said, bowing her head.

For some reason, mom put a hand to her mouth, an astonished look on her face. "Anos... My little Anos..." Then the words came tumbling out. "My little Anos has brought home a BRIDE!!!"

Her voice echoed through the house.

Misha cocked her head. "Does she mean me?"

"Ah, sorry about that. Mom tends to jump to conclusions."

The misunderstanding was a little more dramatic this time, though.

"I see..."

"It's fine, Anos. As long as you're happy, mom is happy as well. I won't hold you back." Mom sniffed, wiping the tears from her eyes.

Just what was going on in mom's head right now? I was too afraid to ask.

"Sorry to dampen your spirits, mom, but..."

The door to the workshop slammed open. "Good job, Anos! That's my boy!"

Ugh, not dad too. Why were these two so excitable?

"I remember the day you were born as if it were yesterday..." Dad assumed a dramatic pose, gazing nostalgically out of the window. "I knew the day would come eventually, but it feels like it's been no time at all." He chuckled heartily.

Of course it felt short; after all, only a month had passed.

"What an auspicious day. Izabella, prepare for a feast. We're going to celebrate!"

"Yes, dear, I know. Our little boy is starting a new chapter of his life."

Dad grinned from ear to ear, and mom wiped away more tears. Then, the two of them faced each other and nodded vigorously.

Misha looked at me. "Does your father jump to conclusions too?"

"I apologize. It's as you can see."

"Right!" dad exclaimed. "Now that's decided, let's get cooking. Come on, Izabella. Give us a smile!"

"You're right—I shouldn't be crying on Anos's big day. It's okay. I can still smile!"

Without another glance at the two of us, mom and dad continued working each other up.

"Say, mom, dad..."

"Oh, don't worry yourself, Anos," dad interrupted. "You don't have to help today—we've got this under control."

An interesting response, all things considered—I'd never helped make dinner in my life.

"Go on then, son. Let's go show Misha your room."

With dad pushing me from behind, we headed upstairs and stopped in front of my room. Just before closing the door, dad turned to me with a glint in his eye.

"Listen up, Anos. Dinner will be ready in two hours. I'll make sure to distract your mother so she doesn't notice any loud noises coming from up here."

Dear father, what are you implying?

"Say, dad—"

"Relax, my boy. You can leave things like this to your good ol' dad!"

The door shut before I could correct him, but not before he could suggestively add, "Have fun!" Good grief, dad sure could be a handful.

"Sorry about this, Misha. I'll explain things to them once they calm down."

"Okay." Misha seemed as fearless as she'd said she was, entirely unaffected by the situation. She surveyed the room with her vacant expression. "It's so empty…"

"We just moved here." That said, I didn't plan on adding much more to it. "You don't really mind, do you?"

"Mind what?"

"How loud mom and dad can be."

"I'm used to it."

I recalled the person who had sent Misha off this morning. "Right, your dad seemed similar."

"Um, no…"

"Oh, sorry. I guess he can't be as bad as mine."

Misha shook her head. "He's not my dad…"

"The person who saw you off this morning wasn't your father?"

Misha shook her head. "He's my guardian."

"Then where are your parents?"

"They're busy…"

Hmm. So that could happen as well. I'd never had a guardian before my reincarnation, but I had been without parents.

"Do you have siblings, Anos?"

"I don't. Why do you ask?"

"'Siblings should get along'…"

"What I said to Zepes and Leorg?"

Misha nodded. "It was kind of you."

"Me?" I couldn't help but burst into laughter.

"Was it that funny?"

"No, it was just the first time I've been called kind."

Misha looked puzzled. "What are you normally called?"

"Let's see..." I thought back on my past life. "'Your existence brings no good,' 'Die for the sake of everyone, you fiend.' 'You ogre,' 'You brute,' 'Do you really have blood flowing in your veins, you monster?'—I've been told many such things and more."

Misha stared at me. "Were you bullied?"

"Me? No way." I had done what was necessary, so I'd brought it upon myself. I had no intention of making excuses. "I was the one at fault."

But despite my clear denial, Misha was concerned. "It wasn't your fault, Anos... The bullies were in the wrong."

"No, but it was—"

Misha stretched up and patted my head gently. "There, there."

Hmm. It seemed she'd misunderstood something. How embarrassing.

"Fine, let's not talk about bullying. What part of me is kind? Those guys earlier sure wouldn't agree."

Zepes had immediately burned his brother to ashes, after all.

"That was just the outcome."

"You think?"

Misha nodded. "Anos is kind."

It was surprisingly nice to hear that for once.

"Do you have siblings, Misha?"

She thought for a brief moment before answering. "I have an older sister..."

"Are you close with her?"

Misha fell briefly silent. "I don't know..."

She didn't know? That was an odd answer. You're either close or you're not... Unless there were more complicated circumstances involved.

"Are you worried about me?" she asked.

"Somewhat."

"So kind."

I thought she might say more about her sister, but Misha merely smiled a little. After that, our casual conversation continued until dinner was ready.

§ 9. Demon King's Friend

Having been called down to eat, Misha and I moved to the dining room. The table was laid with an array of lavish dishes, including my favorite, mushroom gratin.

"Let's all dig in!" mom said, dividing the gratin into several servings.

Phew. I could never get enough of this delectable scent. I was going to start drooling at any moment.

"Here you are, Misha. Eat up."

"Okay…"

Not to brag, but mom's cooking was exquisite. Nothing I'd eaten in the Mythical Age could compare to this. Magic may have declined in this peaceful world, but cooking had evolved in its place—that was the conclusion I'd reached after eating mom's cooking for the past month.

"Thanks for the meal." I scooped the gratin onto my spoon, pausing as it reached my lips. "This is…!"

What?! This gratin had three types of mushrooms in it! King oyster mushrooms, button mushrooms, and porcini mushrooms. She normally used only one variety!

Mom smiled, guessing my thoughts. "I might have splurged a bit. Now go on, eat up."

I nodded, taking a bite of the gratin. "Wuh…!"

It was delicious… The creamy taste melted over my tongue—salty with a hint of sweetness. The rich umami flavor was concentrated into a single mouthful, sinking into the depths of my stomach. The texture of the mushrooms was a perfect contrast to the cream, making me wish I could eat it forever. Ah, reincarnation was truly the best.

"He he. My little Anos has grown up fast, but he still looks like a baby when he eats!" mom cooed.

I was reincarnated, though. I've never been a baby, I thought, too absorbed in eating to reply out loud.

"By the way, there's something I wanted to ask…" mom began, suddenly serious. "What was it that made you fall for our Anos, Misha?"

"Ack—hah…!" I choked with all my might. How careless of me.

"Oh my! Are you okay, Anos?" mom asked.

"Y-Yeah…"

Who could have imagined that I, of all people, would get gratin down the wrong pipe? Mom's gratin was so delicious, I had completely forgotten to clear things up with mom and dad. It had power enough to make even a Demon King lose his composure… How truly fearsome. Perhaps the only one who could defeat me in this era was mom.

"So, what was it…?" mom repeated.

Misha pondered with a blank expression before deciding on her answer. "He's kind…"

The instant Misha gave her matter-of-fact answer, mom clenched her fists. "Ah, yes! That's right! Our Anos is such a good boy! You know, he was going to come to Dilhade alone at first, but when he found out we'd be lonely without him, he brought us along with him! Isn't that right?"

Hmm, I see. This must be what they called the care of an overly doting parent. It was my first time experiencing it, but it was nevertheless embarrassing.

"Filial piety…" Misha murmured.

"Yup, yup! Isn't it wonderful? You sure do get it, Misha! As expected of the one chosen by Anos!"

All right, now was my chance. It was time to correct her.

"Hey, mom—"

"Oh, Anos dear, would you like seconds?"

"What? There's still gratin left? Yes please."

Mom served me more gratin, which I dug into intently. "So, how did you two hit it off?"

"Hit it off...?" Misha repeated.

"How did you meet? Who made the first move?"

"Anos spoke first."

"That's my little boy! Actively approaching girls by himself, this lady-killer!" Mom cat-called with a whistle.

Just what was she talking about?

"So what did Anos say to you?"

Misha looked towards the ceiling, recalling the words I'd said to her. "He said, 'We both have it tough, huh?'"

"Awwww, how sweet! What was that, Anos?! Any girl would fall head over heels for a line like that!"

I didn't see what was so sweet about it, but there was nothing I could say that could get through to this doting parent. I decided to wait a little longer. After all, there was still some gratin left. I had to eat it while it was still hot.

"And? How did you respond, Misha?"

"I said, 'Yeah...'"

"Aww, a telepathic connection! Perfect compatibility from the get-go! A fated love..." Mom was lost in her own dream world and showed no sign of leaving it any time soon. "Then, then, um... Have you two already kissed?"

Hmm. Perhaps this was the perfect chance to explain the situation. Not even mom would believe we were lovers if we'd never kissed before.

"We haven't..."

"Awwwww! Saving it for marriage? How romantic!"

Curses, so there was still that option.

"But what are we to do? Anos is still only one month old. It'll be some time before he's old enough to get married."

"One month...?"

"Yes, isn't it amazing? Anos is such a clever boy, he could talk from the moment he was born. He used a spell called Kurst to grow big and strong!"

Misha eyed me closely. It was exceedingly rare for demons to use magic at one month of age. In other words, my age was proof I'd reincarnated, but it probably wasn't enough to prove I was the Demon King. After all, no one had expected me to reincarnate as a baby.

"Oh? What's wrong, Misha? Does the age gap bother you?"

Of course, mom was thinking about something completely irrelevant as usual.

"It doesn't."

"I-I see... A younger husband is nice as well, right? Anos is a real cutie-pie, after all!"

Misha turned to me. "Cutie-pie...?"

"Don't look at me like that."

That exchange had my mom swinging both fists up and down.

"Awaaaaaaah! Honey, did you hear that?! 'Cutie-pie...?' 'Don't look at me like that.' How cuuute! Are they an old married couple already?!" Mom continued squealing, getting excited all by herself. Dad was enjoying his liquor in silence, gazing into the distance and nodding.

I'd expected them to calm down eventually, but mom's state of excitement continued over the whole of dinner. She talked on and on without a single breath, leaving me with no chance of correcting her.

Thus, dinner was over before I could intervene. We continued chatting late into the night until Misha had to head home. I accompanied her outside to send her off.

"Misha, give me your hand."

She offered it to me obediently.

"I'll send you home with Gatom."

"But you don't know where to…"

"Picture your house. I'll read it from your thoughts."

"You can do that?"

"Naturally."

Misha stared at me. "Impressive."

The location of Misha's house was transmitted to my mind through our linked hands.

"I'm sorry about today."

Misha shook her head. "It was fun."

"That's good. Once mom and dad have calmed down, I'll explain that we're comrades."

"Comrades?"

"Ah, right. In this era, that would be friends."

Misha pointed to herself. "I'm your friend?"

"Was I wrong? What would you call this relationship, then?"

Misha shook her head, then smiled sweetly. "I'm happy."

"I see."

"Yeah…"

I sent magic to my hand to activate Gatom.

"See you at school, Misha."

"Goodbye."

Misha's body disappeared, teleported away.

§ 10. Brand of the Misfit

Several days later.

Having donned the uniform that had been sent via owl, I made my way to Delsgade. Today was the first day of school. Many students were passing through the front gate, heading into the grounds.

At a glance, I could distinguish two types of uniform. The one I wore was white, but there was also a black version, with students divided into roughly a fifty-fifty split. Whether a student wore one or the other didn't seem determined by school year.

The insignias on our school badges also differed. Mine was a cross, but others bore triangles, squares, and five- and six-pointed stars. There were no other crosses in sight.

But what were all the strange looks for? It was as if anyone who noticed me was staring in curiosity. This hadn't been the case during the entrance exam… Well, there was no point thinking about it. If there was a problem, I'd soon find out.

Inside the school grounds was a large bulletin board. It listed the names of new students, divided into classes. The name Anos Voldigoad appeared under the column for class two. Mom and dad's last name was Raizeo, but we'd had the opportunity to apply for a demon surname when we moved to Dilhade, so I, of course, chose Voldigoad. Mom and dad had also adopted the name here.

After confirming that class two was in the second lecture hall, I walked through the castle's familiar corridors and up a flight of stairs towards the classroom. When I got there, I opened the door and went inside. Desks and chairs were lined up in rows, and the students all turned to face me.

Hmm. Yes, this attention was rather odd.

But, well, these people were about to become my classmates. I wasn't familiar with these kinds of situations, but I had heard that first impressions are the most important. This was my chance to leave the impression of a friendly compeer.

With a beaming smile and the most energetic voice I could muster, I called out to those around me. "Greetings, fellow classmates! I have come to reign over this class! Any soul who dares defy me will meet their immediate demise!"

Heh. That should do it.

For some reason, my ardent greeting was met by a chilling silence. Had my voice lacked clarity? Was I, of all people, much too eager on my first day of school?

But amongst the terrified eyes fixed upon me, there was one gaze as undaunted as ever. It was a girl with platinum-blonde hair, dressed in a white uniform—Misha.

I walked over to her seat.

"Hey," I said.

Misha looked at me with no particular emotion. "Good morning."

"Is this seat free?"

"Yeah."

I pulled out the chair and sat down beside her, taking the chance to ask her the question on my mind. "How was my joke just now?"

Misha looked puzzled. "Joke...?"

"To kill anyone who defies me."

There was no way anyone would think I was serious. The joke had been the height of hilarity for all back in the Mythical Age. My subordinates would always come back at me with a hearty, "Y-You jest..." in response.

"I think you were misunderstood..."

Ugh, right. This was a different era. I'd decided to restrain my humor after the fiasco at the entrance exam, but my mouth had moved before I could stop myself.

"Should I have held off until after settling into the class?"

"Yeah..."

That aside, I could still feel their gazes.

"By the way, I can't help but feel as though I'm being watched. It's been that way for some time now. Do you know why?"

"There are rumors."

"About me? What kind of rumors?"

"You won't get mad...?"

"Despite appearances, I've never been one to anger."

"That symbol..." Misha pointed to my badge. "It represents the results of the last test."

"Oh, I see. How does that work?"

"The more vertices on the polygon or star, the better."

So, correlating with our test results, a square was better than a triangle, and a pentagram was better than a square.

"But my symbol is a cross, not a star."

It wasn't a triangle or square either.

"You're the first to be marked with that symbol in the history of the academy. It's a brand..."

A brand? Hmm. Was that something bad?

"What does it mean?"

"Misfit," Misha said plainly. "The Demon King Academy exists to train demon lords. Only descendants of the founder are permitted to attend."

In my spare time before school had started, I'd done some research on this era. "Demon King" was a title reserved for me alone, but there were other important figures in this age known as demon "lords," who all had one thing in common: the blood of the founder.

"Until now," Misha continued, "no descendant has been ruled to have zero demon lord aptitude. You're the first misfit." She paused. "That's why people are talking."

Hmm. I had no idea how they determined this so-called demon lord aptitude, but the fact they had branded their very own founder a misfit meant their examination method was fatally flawed. I'd expected them to discover me as soon as I enrolled, but it seemed, once again, that the demons of this era were less capable than I'd thought.

"I understand they were unable to measure the immensity of my power, but my aptitude test should have been flawless."

"You're confident...?"

"Yeah."

The questions had all been about myself, the founding ancestor—my name, my attitude towards things, and so on. There was no way I'd get them wrong...

Wait.

"Say, Misha. Would you say the founder's name?"

Misha blinked at me. "The name of the founding ancestor is too fear-invoking to be spoken aloud."

"What's my name?"

"Anos?" Misha said, puzzled.

"My full name?"

"Anos Voldigoad."

I see.

"May I?" I placed my hand on Misha's head.

She didn't seem particularly bothered by it but looked at me curiously. "What's wrong?"

"Think of the founder's name."

"Okay..."

The next moment, I read the name from Misha's mind.

The Demon King of Tyranny, Avos Dilhevia.

"Who...?"

"Is something wrong?"

"It's the wrong name."

Misha shook her head. "It can't be. No demon would ever get it wrong."

"And the founder's name is too fearsome to say aloud, right?"

Misha nodded.

"I see."

In other words, thanks to everyone being too afraid to speak the founder's name, demonkind had, over the course of two thousand years, slowly forgotten it. The wrong name had been passed down instead. How preposterous.

Now I thought about it, Leorg had said he was risking his life to cast origin magic. Calling upon an origin with the wrong name would indeed endanger his life!

If even my name had been misremembered, the other answers on the aptitude test couldn't have fared better. My sleepy casting of Jio Graze without causing any casualties had probably been forgotten as well.

But in that case, where had my subordinates gone? Had they discarded their memories and reincarnated? Perhaps they were in the middle of the reincarnation process. At any rate, it had been two thousand years. There were many possibilities.

"How is aptitude for demon lords decided?"

"Demons with similar thoughts and beliefs to the Demon King have higher aptitude."

"I see. Then what kind of demon was the Demon King of Tyranny said to be?"

"He was a perfect existence: a balance of cruelty and benevolence. He cared only for demonkind and fought without concern for himself.

He had no greed, a noble heart, and the reasons for his tyranny were beyond the understanding of others."

Who in the world was that? As if such an idyllic man could exist. Fools. It was natural to exaggerate legends and folktales, but why would one believe these tales word for word?

Considering the state of this mess, it was no wonder I'd been branded a misfit. By their standards, I didn't even know my own name.

"I understand the meaning of the brand now, but why the two different uniforms?"

As was the case outside, half the students in the class wore black uniforms, the other half wore white.

"The black uniforms are for the elite—pure-blooded descendants commonly referred to as 'royals.'"

"Like Leorg?"

"Yeah."

Those who inherited my blood were known as descendants. Distinguishing them between pure- and mixed-blood was a little strange, but the foundations of the belief were simple. Two thousand years ago, I had used my blood to magically create seven demons, who in turn had used their blood to create more descendants. Like this, the number of demons descended purely from my blood had increased until they could naturally produce pure-blooded children without magic.

"The elite are exempt from entrance exams."

"So why was that guy taking the test?"

"Anyone who wants to can take it."

I see. So those who wanted to show off their power could take the practical test if they wished. No wonder there had only been weaklings there. The truly powerful had no need for such pointless shows.

Just then, a bell rang in the distance.

"Please take your seats, everyone."

I looked up as a woman in a black robe entered the classroom. She wrote something on the blackboard with magic.

Emilia Ludwell.

"My name is Emilia, and I shall be the homeroom teacher for class two. Pleasure to meet you all."

Hmm. At least the teaching staff possessed sufficient magic. Leorg wouldn't stand a chance against her.

"Let's get straight to it. First, you will all be split into teams. Anyone who wishes to be a team leader, please nominate yourselves. The only condition is that you are able to cast the spell I am about to show you."

The lesson began abruptly with Emilia drawing a magic circle on the blackboard. The board seemed custom made—a magic item of some sort. By sending magic power along its surface, letters could be written and magic circles could be drawn.

This circle was for Gyze.

"I'm sure this is your first time seeing it, but this spell is called Gyze. To put it simply, it treats the caster as a king and bestows special powers upon their subordinates. You'll have a chance to practice this in class. Today, we shall be working on drawing the circle and casting the spell. Those who do so successfully will qualify as team leader."

Considering the peculiarities of Gyze, only those who became a team leader here would have the qualities to pursue the path of a demon lord.

"Now, if the nominees could please raise their hands."

I did so without hesitation.

My peers were all incompetent demons who couldn't recognize their own founder, but I wouldn't criticize them too harshly. In the end, they were my descendants—part of the responsibility lay with me.

Even if they couldn't see it now, all I had to do was prove my abilities. That said, the reactions from my classmates were as unfavorable as ever. They were staring at me with shocked expressions.

Good grief. Misfit or not, nominating myself as team leader hardly warranted this kind of reaction.

"Those in white can't be nominated," Misha informed me in a quiet voice. Everyone else with their hands up wore black uniforms—in other words, only pure-blooded demons could apply. How ridiculous.

"Anos, was it?" Emilia asked with a conflicted smile. "I'm afraid you're not qualified."

"Why not?"

"Because you're of mixed blood."

"Mixed blood doesn't imply inferiority to purebloods."

As I said that, Emilia frowned. "Are you prejudiced against royalty?"

Why did these fools keep saying such things?

"What nonsense. Instead of this incessant blabbering, why don't you prove that purebloods are superior? If you cannot, then I'll be nominating myself."

Emilia sighed. "I should be the one saying that. Our founder, the Demon King, already proved as much. If half-breeds are as superior as you say, then *you* should prove you can win against royalty."

"Hmm. So if I can do that, I'll be able to nominate myself?"

"If you can, then be my guest."

I chuckled. "I'll seal those words with *Zecht*."

"Wh-Wha… When did you cast that?"

Using Zecht to seal a verbal promise had been commonplace in the Mythical Age. Her failure to notice the spell indicated her failure as a teacher.

At any rate, I stood up and walked over to the blackboard. "Was it demon royalty that developed Gyze?"

"Yes."

Of course it was. I had developed it, after all.

"There's a flaw in the spell circle."

"What? Impossible. The formula for Gyze has been passed down for two thousand years without alterations. No one has ever found a flaw in it."

"I found it myself two thousand years ago, but I died before I could fix it." I redrew three sections of the circle. "This is the completed form. If you're a teacher, you should be able to tell by looking at it, correct?"

Emilia stared in disbelief at the magic circle. "How... With just three corrections, you've improved its efficiency by ten percent—and its effect by fifteen? That's...!"

The classroom stirred.

"Who the hell is this guy...?"

"He identified a flaw in a magic circle he's never seen before, and then he fixed it? I've never heard of such a thing! We haven't even started learning the fundamentals of magic research..."

"On top of that, he increased its efficiency and effect..."

"This has to be the discovery of the century..."

Hmm. Their standards must be low to be impressed by so little. Not to mention...

"You're close, but still wrong," I told Emilia.

She turned to me, uncomprehending.

"The effectiveness is now double what it was. This magic gate interacts with these three magic runes, causing the entire thing to resonate with the source twice."

"Ah..." Realization finally dawned on Emilia, who shrank back in embarrassment.

"If you'd like, I can teach this class in your place."

"Y-You..."

"Hmm?"

"You may nominate yourself. Now please return to your seat," was all Emilia was able to say.

§ 11. Witch of Destruction

Once I'd returned to my seat, Emilia continued speaking.

"Nominees, please rise."

The students who had raised their hands earlier stood up. There were four demons, excluding myself. I wasn't particularly interested in the competition, but when I glanced over the candidates, my eyes stopped on a girl—a girl with blue eyes and blonde twintails. Her expression portrayed a fierce tenacity, yet there was something about her face and stature that reminded me of Misha. Above all, the wavelengths of their magic were identical.

"We shall now begin the team allocations. First, the students nominated as team leaders will introduce themselves. Sasha, if you would start us off."

The twintailed girl smiled smugly. "Very well. I am Sasha Necron, the Witch of Destruction, a member of the Necron family, and a direct descendant of the Demon Elder Ivis Necron. Pleased to meet you all."

She pinched the hem of her skirt and curtsied gracefully.

Misha, who had been listening to the class absentmindedly until now, had her gaze fixed intently on the girl.

I turned to her. "If she's a Necron, then..."

"She's my older sister."

I see. So this was the sister she didn't know if she was close with. Sasha wore a black uniform, so she had to be pure-blooded, but Misha wore white. That meant...

"You're half sisters?" I asked, but Misha shook her head.

"We have the same parents."

"Shouldn't you be a pureblood, then?"

"There are other reasons for wearing white."

"Such as?"

Misha fell silent for a moment, then answered. "My family decided it..."

"Your family?"

"The Necron family."

Hmm. What kind of circumstances would make you treat one pure-blood daughter like royalty, but not the other? It seemed rather unnatural for this era, in which lineage was valued above all else.

Emilia's voice interrupted my thoughts. "It's your turn, Anos."

Apparently, my turn had come while I'd been talking to Misha. Well, I could just ask her later.

First came the self-introduction. I faced the other students and grandly declared, "My name is Anos Voldigoad, Demon King of Tyranny. I must warn you, the name you all believe to be that of the Demon King is no more than a forgery. The true name you seek is Anos Voldigoad. I'm aware you won't believe me, but that's all right. You'll come to realize your ignorance with time. It's a pleasure."

My introduction was greeted by silence so abundant, one could hear a pin drop. As Leorg had said, proclaiming oneself the founder was both commonplace and blasphemous. All the more so when accusing the name that had been passed down through the generations of being a lie.

Everyone was glancing my way and whispering amongst themselves, saying this and that about me being a misfit. It should have been Emilia's job to quiet them, but after what had happened earlier, she seemed content to ignore them and continue her explanation.

"That concludes the introductions. Those of you who weren't nominated, please move to the leader you would like to join. I know you're still unfamiliar with one another, so judging by first impressions is fine. There's no limit to the number of people in a team, so groups can be as large as you wish."

With that, the students stood up and each made their way over to their preferred team leader.

"You may change teams whenever you like. However, it is up to the leader whether they wish to let you in. In the event there are no members left in the team, the leader loses their right to lead."

So this was a test of one's capabilities as a leader. The rest of the class began to talk again, deciding for themselves who they thought most capable.

"Hey, what are you gonna do?"

"I'm joining Lady Sasha's team, of course."

"Right? The Witch of Destruction is a top contender in the Cohort of Chaos. Rumor has it she's the reincarnated founder."

"Yeah, I've heard those rumors too. She has a tremendous amount of magic power."

Hmm. So this Sasha girl was one of the Cohort of Chaos. Of course, she wasn't the founder—that was me—but she must possess considerable magic to be rumored as such. As evidence of that, the majority of the class was moving to join her team.

Misha stood up beside me. For a brief moment, she glanced blankly in Sasha's direction, then looked back at me.

"You can join your sister if you'd like."

Misha shook her head. "I want to join your team."

"Really?"

"Yeah."

"That'd be great."

Misha blushed faintly. "Because we're friends..."

"That we are."

Thanks to that, I now had one team member. We were officially a team, but what next? I could easily gather more members with magic, but that was no fun at all. As I thought about it, the crowd of students parted to let a blonde-haired girl pass.

It was Sasha.

"Good day. Anos Voldigoad, was it?"

"Yes."

She glanced at Misha. "I see you only have one team member. You must be out of your mind to let a defective doll like her onto your team."

Hmm. If this girl was looking to pick a fight with *me*, then *she* was out of *her* mind.

"By defective doll, are you referring to Misha?"

"Who else?" Sasha giggled mockingly, as if to look down on me. "Don't you know? The girl isn't a demon. But she isn't a human either. She's a defective doll with no life, no soul, and no will of her own—a worthless puppet animated by magic."

So Misha was some kind of magic doll? She'd said they shared the same parents, but had she been created magically from their blood instead? Well, there were an infinite number of ways to create magical constructs—there were even some that could be created by giving birth. A well-made doll could be as alive as the rest of us.

"What of it?"

"What of...?"

"If you believe a magic doll is lifeless and has no soul of its own, then you have an awfully shallow understanding of magic. You should look more carefully into the abyss with those *Eyes* of yours."

Sasha looked surprised for a brief moment, but then smirked daringly anyway. "I'm just giving you a warning. If you stick with that cursed puppet, something *bad* may happen. You get what I'm saying, don't you?"

I snorted. "What, is that a threat? You think you can threaten *me*?"

Suddenly, Sasha glared at me, magic circles lighting her blue eyes. "Hey. Do you have a death wish?"

The students that had been watching until now began murmuring amongst themselves.

"That guy's done for. He's looked into Lady Sasha's Eyes for too long..."

"What do you mean?"

"Don't you know? Lady Sasha's Eyes are special. They're called the Magic Eyes of Destruction; she can make anything she looks at self-destruct. It's the reason she's known as the Witch of Destruction."

So it was a unique constitution. Be it Misha or Sasha, the Necron family sure had some powerful Eyes. However, they had no effect on me.

"That can't be..." Sasha murmured.

"What's wrong? Giving up on our staring contest?" I glared back at her. By sending magic power to my own eyes, I drew the familiar formula on my pupils.

"Those Eyes... There's no way! You..."

"What? There's nothing you can do that I cannot. But I'll let you in on a little something—you're using them incorrectly."

Sasha was on the right track, but her practical application was still lacking. For the sake of her education, I might as well correct her.

"Let me show you. *These* are the true Magic Eyes of Destruction."

"Ah... Ahh..."

Not a single object in the classroom was destroyed. At first glance, Sasha also appeared unharmed. What I had destroyed was that arrogant attitude of hers.

"I can't believe it. He's fine after looking Lady Sasha in the eye..."

"The last time I accidentally looked into them when they were activated, I was put into a coma for a year..."

"What's happening? Isn't that white uniform guy a misfit? How can he be so knowledgeable about spells and have that kind of magic resistance?"

Hmm. The classroom was getting rather noisy.

"Actually, I was told not to tell anyone this, but I saw his entrance exam. In the practical, he killed Duke Leorg in an instant..."

"What?! A demon duke was killed *instantly*?!"

"Before that, he killed Zepes too."

"He killed him? For real?!"

"Yeah. Then he revived him."

"Revived?!"

"And then killed him again."

"You don't say..."

"After that, Zepes turned into a zombie and burned Duke Leorg to death."

"Th-That's..."

"Huh? But I saw Duke Leorg after the entrance exam..."

"He ended up reviving the two of them."

"What in the world...?"

Well, let's leave it at that.

"For how long will you remain dazed? I only destroyed the outer layer of your heart. Pull yourself together." I patted Sasha's head gently, waking her mind.

She gasped, and her eyes fixed on mine. "Who...are you...?"

"I introduced myself earlier, didn't I?" I said, grinning.

She glared back in frustration.

"By the way, Sasha, you're fairly gifted with magic. How would you like to join my team?"

Apparently, those were the last words she'd expected, as she fell completely speechless.

§ 12. Gyze Magic

"Wh-What are you saying? You make no sense…"

When Sasha finally refound her voice, it was to utter something so trifling.

"I'm inviting you onto my team. What's so hard to understand?"

"That's not what I'm saying. I'm a team leader, you know?"

"You can quit."

"Excuse me?!" Sasha's mouth fell open in shock. She looked at me in disgust. "Don't be ridiculous. I have no reason to quit."

"If you join my team, you'll get to be with Misha."

My words seemed to touch a nerve—Sasha's glare grew harsher, and she spun around to leave. "I've never thought of that doll as my sister. Not even once," she snapped, returning to her seat.

"I'm sorry," Misha muttered beside me.

"There's no need to apologize. She was the one picking the fight."

Misha shook her head. "Sasha's a good girl…"

I couldn't tell if she was protecting her sister or if she truly thought that way. Her lack of expression made her hard to read.

"That's why it's my fault."

Hmm. She didn't seem to have any hard feelings about being called a worthless puppet, at least.

"Then let me rephrase. It's nice to see your sister is spirited enough to try to kill me with her Eyes. No one's at fault."

Misha stared at me. "How kind."

That said, there was something I was curious about.

"What did she mean by 'doll'?"

Misha fell briefly silent, making no attempt to answer. "Do I have to say...?"

So she didn't want to talk about it. Well, it didn't really matter. Magic doll or not, Misha was my friend.

"No. I was just wondering."

She smiled, clearly relieved. "Okay."

Just then, our teacher clapped her together, calling the attention of the class.

"All right, now the teams are decided, let's continue. Please return to your seats."

The students sat down as per Emilia's orders.

"For the time being, this class will focus on Gyze. Practical experience is especially vital when it comes to this spell, so we'll be holding a team exam in a week's time. Keep that in mind as you study."

With that, Emilia launched into an explanation about Gyze and its use in the exam.

Gyze was a type of military magic that could boost the combat abilities of one's troops on a battlefield. It was a little different than other spells in that it classified each recipient, the caster and their subordinates, into one of seven classes: King, Guardian, Mage, Healer, Summoner, Cavalier, or Shaman.

The effect of the spell was unique for each class. For example, Guardians were granted creation magic to construct castles and dungeons, defense magic to erect walls and magic barriers, and general magic enhancement. On the other hand, their weapon magic and attack magic is severely weakened. This class system allowed Gyze to raise the overall power of one's army.

The caster is always the King. They have the ability to share their magic power, but have to keep the magic constantly activated. Naturally, once they run out of power or die, Gyze's effects end.

"Now, we shall first assess whether the team leader nominees can cast Gyze successfully."

If any of the nominees failed to cast the spell, their team members would be equally humiliated for their poor judgment.

Each of the nominees took turns casting Gyze, and all of the five leaders succeeded. Honestly though, none of them were at a level that would deem them useful in real battle, with the exception of Sasha. Her casting was exceptionally stable—as expected of one of the Cohort of Chaos.

"Right, that's enough. I shall now explain the details of Gyze. First…"

Emilia resumed the lesson. However, since I was the one who had developed this spell, I was already aware of the details. Moreover, some of the things she said were clearly wrong, but there'd be no end to the lesson if I tried to correct her. It was best to let her comments slide.

Bored to death by the tedious class, I drifted off to sleep.

Eventually, interrupting my slumber, the sound of the bell signaled the end of the lesson.

"Misha." The snappy voice filled my ears. It was Sasha. "Could you pass on a message to him?"

A message, when I'm right here?

"Should I wake him…?"

"No need."

I thought she'd get straight to the point, but for some reason, a silence followed.

"Say, what is he to you?" Sasha asked her sister.

After a pause, Misha replied. "My friend."

"I see. Are you having fun?"

"Yeah…"

"Hmm. Good for you."

Sasha's tone was still harsh, but there was a part of her that seemed happy. Misha didn't seem to hate her either. This really was a relationship on neither good nor bad terms. Was there a reason behind that worthless puppet comment? I suppose even sisters fight from time to time.

"So what's the message?" I asked.

"Eek!" Sasha flinched back in shock. "D-Did you have to wake up like that? You scared me."

"You can't tell if I'm awake from the flow of magic? Pathetic."

She glared at me in silent anger.

"So, what do you want?"

The Magic Eyes of Destruction glowed in Sasha's pupils. From what I could see, it was a natural reaction to a dramatic change in her emotions—in other words, she couldn't control them herself. Despite that, her Magic Eyes were an enchanting sight to see. Their beauty was a reflection of her talent.

"Let's make a wager," she proposed.

That was an unexpected suggestion. Two thousand years ago, barely anyone, be they demon or human, had been bold enough to utter such words to me.

"Me and you? What kind of wager?" I chuckled. No matter the challenge, there was no way I would lose.

"Ms. Emilia said there's a team competition next week. What if the loser of that match has to do as the victor says?"

"Sounds interesting."

"If you win, I'll quit my team and join yours."

"And if you win?"

Sasha smiled. "You'll be mine."

"You want me to join your team?"

"No. You'll cut ties with that doll and become mine. You'll obey my every order without a word of complaint." Sasha looked down on her sister with a smirk. "Remember, Misha. Everything that's yours belongs to me. You're not allowed anything, not even a single friend. Such an intriguing toy is wasted on you anyway."

Good grief. She may have been acting out of spite, but she sure had guts to treat me like a plaything.

"I'm fine with that."

"Oh? That was easy. Are you sure?"

"Yeah. I'm going to win either way."

Sasha scowled at me. "I let my guard down earlier, but you'd better be ready for next week," she said.

Then, with a flip of her skirt, she spun around and left.

"Once you're on the same team, maybe you can make up," I suggested to Misha, who blinked in surprise.

"Is that why you invited her?"

"Was it too meddlesome of me?"

Misha shook her head, then smiled faintly. "Thank you."

My hunch was correct after all—Misha did want to get closer to Sasha. Things didn't seem so simple for her sister, but I'm sure it'd work out.

"No worries. Let's do our best in the exam."

Misha nodded. "I'll try..."

§ 13. Team Exam

One week later.

Awaiting their exam, the students of class two had gathered at the enchanted forest behind the academy. Eerie-looking trees grew as far as the eye could see, over the sides of valleys and mountains. The vast space was most suitable for holding practical magic lessons.

"Let's get straight to it," Emilia called out. "I shall select two teams to go first. Team Sasha—" Sasha stepped forward "—set an example for everyone."

"I understand," she said with a smile.

"Now, the opposing team will be..."

Sasha glared at me. She didn't have to look so intense—I wasn't about to run away.

"I'll face her." I stepped forward with Misha.

"Then the exam will commence with Team Sasha and Team Anos. The results will affect your grades, so make sure you put in a proper effort."

With that, Emilia left the forest with the remaining students. The match would probably be monitored through a familiar or Great Mirror.

Team competitions that involved the use of Gyze were, in essence, mock wars. Getting caught in the crossfire could lead to serious injuries.

"I hope you're ready." Sasha glared at me confidently, her Magic Eyes ablaze.

I met them with my gaze. "Who do you think you're talking to?"

"How arrogant. You'd better remember our promise."

"Of course," I said.

"I don't trust your words."

"The same goes for me."

I tried to cast Zecht, but Sasha refused and canceled it.

"But you just said you don't trust me," I remarked.

"Who knows what kind of tricks you'll use to manipulate our contract?"

Hmm. Despite me being a misfit, Sasha wasn't underestimating me. It seemed she, too, could see the abyss clearly.

"Have her cast it instead." Sasha directed her gaze to Misha, who was standing behind me. She returned her sister's stare quietly, unmoved by her destructive gaze.

"Is that okay...?" she asked, looking to me for reassurance.

"Yeah," I said. "It doesn't matter who casts it."

Misha held out her hand and cast the circle for Zecht. Its magic runes listed the conditions of our contract. Sasha and I signed it. Without the mutual agreement of both sides to dissolve it, the contract was absolute.

"Which position do you want?" Sasha then asked.

"You can decide. It won't make a difference."

"Really. Then I'll take the east."

That left the west for me.

"Hey," she added. "Watch that attitude of yours. Or I'll make you regret it."

Sasha turned in a huff and headed towards the forest's east side, closely followed by her team.

"We should get going too," I told Misha.

"Yeah."

We started walking, eventually arriving at the west side of the forest. There we waited, until...

"Looks like it's about time."

The owl flying overhead began broadcasting a message using Leaks.

"The team exam between Team Sasha and Team Anos will now begin. The use of any magic and items is permitted. The match will end when a King is rendered incapable of combat or maintaining Gyze. The exam must take place within the boundaries of the enchanted forest. Any student caught leaving will be considered to have surrendered. Defeat your enemies in a way the founder would be proud of!"

In a way the founder would be proud of? It wasn't as though I particularly reveled in the defeat of my enemies. The Mythical Age hadn't been as peaceful as this era, so it was merely the most effective way of getting things done. I was a pacifist by nature, but the people of this time seemed to think the opposite. Honestly, if I were as aggressive as they said, there'd be no way I would have stayed silent after being branded a misfit. Well, it wasn't as though it was the first time this had happened.

"What's the plan?" Misha asked.

"There's only two of us. Not much planning we can do."

Sasha's team had thirty people—roughly half the class.

"Any ideas, Misha?" I asked.

She thought for a moment.

I'd already activated Gyze. Any of the spell's classes could be freely assigned to one's subordinates, so I'd made Misha a Guardian since she was good at construction magic. The Guardian class gained a magical boost when constructing castles, dungeons, walls, and barriers. This was further buffed due to me being such a powerful caster of Gyze.

"I can construct a Demon King Castle with Iris. The castle will boost the abilities of the King, making it advantageous in a siege," Misha suggested.

It was a reasonable strategy that would make the most of our strengths.

"But Sasha will be expecting that," I concluded.

"So…what do we do?"

Frankly speaking, there was no point in thinking of a strategy. No matter what I did, there was no way I could lose. That being said, it would be nice to see Sasha's flustered face.

"We'll outsmart the enemy with a strategy they'll never expect."

Misha stared at me. "Like what?"

"The King class becomes weaker when separated from the subordinates sharing his or her magic. The standard move is to build a castle and remain within it for protection."

Kings' powers are greatly enhanced by being inside their castle, but the magnitude of that effect depended on their Guardian.

"That's why we'll use our castle as a decoy while I invade theirs alone."

Misha's expression was unmoving as ever, but her silence made her seem surprised.

"What do you think?"

"Crazy…"

I laughed heartily. "I'm sure the other side will think so too. That's why it'll work."

"Will you be okay?"

"Indeed, a strategy like this would normally result in concentrated spellfire on the King. But that's only if the forces are strong enough for such a tactic to be effective."

Misha still seemed to have some concerns, as her expression remained unchanged.

"Are you worried?" I asked, but she shook her head.

"I'm a little worried, but…you're strong."

At least she understood. Clearly, she could see into the abyss of my source with those Eyes of hers.

"I'll leave the decoys to you."

Misha nodded. "Be careful."

"Yeah, I'll try to go easy on them."

She blinked in confusion. "I meant you."

"Me? You want me to watch out for myself?" I asked, surprised.

Misha tilted her head. "Is that strange...?"

"No," I said with a chuckle.

I never imagined there'd be someone worried about *me* in a battle. Was this what it meant to have friends? What an unfamiliar feeling. It was surprisingly nice though.

"You be careful too, Misha."

"Yeah."

With a wave, I bid Misha farewell and headed straight for the east side, where Sasha's encampment was.

Not long after, a large amount of magic power surged behind me. I turned back to see three large castles standing on the west side of the forest. So this was Misha's magic. They were hollow shells built to act as decoys, but it still took a tremendous amount of magic to build three huge castles in such a short time.

I was better, though.

"Now, let's see how they'll react..."

I activated my Magic Eyes to intercept their Leaks. Their voices immediately reached my ears.

"Lady Sasha. Three castles have been constructed on the enemy camp."

"Two of them must be traps. Their King will be hiding in the real one."

"Shall we destroy each castle one by one?"

"No. Misha can't build a complete Demon King Castle so quickly. She's buying time to construct a sturdier fortress. We have to attack before then."

"Understood. Awaiting your orders."

"Form three squads, each composed of a Cavalier, two Healers, and a Summoner. Each squad will head out to an enemy castle."

"Roger that!"

I see. That meant three squads of a total of twelve people were heading this way, a somewhat defensive move would leave over half her troops in her own encampment. But now—

"Hmm. She's finally constructed her castle," I noted.

It had taken longer than I'd expected, but a huge Demon King Castle had appeared on the enemy field. Even I was unable to move without a destination. But now—*Gatom.*

My vision turned white, and before I knew it, I was standing before Team Sasha's castle. The Leaks I'd intercepted echoed noisily in my head.

"L-Lady Sasha!"

"What's wrong?"

"Th-Their King, Anos Voldigoad, just appeared in front of our castle!"

"Huh?! How in the world?"

"I don't know! Our Shaman was carefully watching the flow of magic on our land, but he appeared out of nowhere! He must have used some kind of magic that we don't know about!"

Sasha gasped. "It couldn't be Gatom, could it…? There's no way. But how else could he have…"

Hmm. Not bad. Realizing what had happened without even seeing it required quite the flexible mind.

"It's fine. Either way, a King moving on his own is just begging to be killed. He might think he's outwitting us, but we'll show him how much of a reckless fool he is!"

"I wouldn't be too sure about that," I said, interrupting them through their Leaks.

Team Sasha began panicking further.

"Wha… What's the meaning of this? How can we hear his voice?!"

"I-I don't know. There's no problem with the magic circle—it should be impossible!"

"But I just heard him! Quick—find out what's going on! He may have intercepted our Leaks!"

Oh my. What a racket.

"The flaw is in your spell formula. That circle only has a recreation ratio of eighty-nine percent—that's so low, it's like you're begging me to intercept it."

Sasha's team remained adamant. "Nonsense! Eighty-nine percent is the same standard as national security channels! There's no way it can be intercepted."

Magic circles must incorporate a spell formula in order to function. These formulae come in two forms—theoretical formulae and practical formulae. Theoretical formulae are the most optimal for spell performance, but in practice, the recreation of a theoretical magic circle can prove difficult. The formula degrades in accordance with its caster and environment, resulting in the aforementioned practical formula. The ratio between the two formulae's effectiveness is the recreation ratio, or efficiency value.

In this era, both theoretical and practical spell formulae were of an abysmal standard. Practical formula aside though, there was little point in pointing out the ideal theoretical formula—it wasn't something that could be understood overnight.

"Don't be fooled by his words!" Team Sasha persisted. "There has to be some other reason!"

So I had kindly informed them of the cause, and this was how they treated me?

"It doesn't matter." Sasha's voice cut through their ruckus, her calm words helping the others regain their composure. The girl certainly had some charisma to her.

"No matter how he intercepted our Leaks, he's still a King who stands alone. Our castle was created by seven Guardians. He wouldn't even be able to break through the first floor."

Seven Guardians, huh? That would make for quite the sturdy build. There must be multiple barriers, traps, and protections to strengthen the King within it. However...

"What a light-looking castle." I walked up to the fortress and placed my hand against the ramparts.

"Give up. We've cast multiple layers of anti-magic."

"Your knowledge of battle is lacking if you only guard against magic." I clenched my fist. My fingers dug into the wall. "Remember this. Castles are meant to be heavy."

The ground rumbled and cracked as the castle was torn from its foundations.

"Wh-What's going on?! Shaman!"

"I can't believe it... He... Anos Voldigoad is lifting the castle!"

"What...? That's impossible!"

Once the castle was completely freed from the ground, I held it up with one hand.

"No way..." Sasha muttered. "How can an unprotected King have so much power?"

"It's true that Gyze can influence the power of a class. But our abilities were never on the same level to begin with."

Pivoting, I slowly turned my body. The castle I held spun with me—round and round, faster and faster as the centrifugal force amassed.

"Huh?! Awaaaaah!"

"I-Is he a monster?! He didn't just pick the castle up—he's spinning it around!"

"Stop! What are you doing?! Stoooop!"

Hmph. Such a pathetic reaction.

Their anti-magic defenses were fine, but they were completely unguarded against physical attacks. To begin with, the demons of this era were so accustomed to peace, they'd neglected to train their bodies.

Before developing spells and formulae for powerful magic, one must first build physical strength. That went for castles too.

"Better brace yourselves for the fall...or you'll die."

I threw the rapidly spinning castle with all my might. The fortress shot through the air, crashing into the ground with a thundering boom.

§ 14. Power of Another Level

"Awaaaaaaah!"

Sasha's scream echoed over the intercepted Leaks.

Hmm. Had I gone too easy on them? There was less damage than I'd expected. The Demon King Castle, which had slammed into the ground, was only half-destroyed. Well, whatever. They were still capable of fighting, so what would they do now?

I unhurriedly made my way over to the ruined castle, listening closely as Sasha came to a decision over their Leaks.

"We'll use Jio Graze," she commanded.

Oh? Intriguing choice.

"B-But Lady Sasha, even with the protection of the castle and the combined power of the Mages, Jio Graze has only a twenty percent chance of success!"

"If you fail, the castle will be destroyed!"

"This is no time for fear! Recognize the strength of our enemy. He may be a hybrid, he may be a misfit—but Anos Voldigoad is a monster capable of throwing an entire castle! Did you think we'd stand a chance with any regular spell?"

The whining team members quieted. Sasha really was a charismatic leader. She still lacked experience, but it was a shame to be on opposing sides.

"Unless we use the highest grade of fire magic, we cannot defeat Anos Voldigoad. Am I wrong?"

There were no objections, but the faint magic power I could feel through the Leaks connection told me of their resolution.

"This is a battle of one against twenty! It'd be a disgrace to lose like this, so fight like your life depends on it. Show that mongrel the best magic you've ever cast. Show him your pride as royalty!"

Sasha's admonishment spurred her team members on.

"Roger!"

The next moment, particles of magic rose around the Demon King Castle, forming a three-dimensional magic circle. The castle itself became the spell circle, to allow for casting greater spells.

The seven Guardians, who had built the castle, constructed and maintained the complex circle while the ten Mages poured all their magic into it. The remaining teammates, two Shamans, were responsible for aiming the spell.

Sasha Necron herself was in charge of assembling the spell formula. Her talent was rare—talent that deemed her worthy of the title Witch of Destruction—yet even with the borrowed power of her team, casting a spell of this scale was no mean feat.

Unlike origin magic, which used a risky springboard to gain immense power, Jio Graze could only be accomplished by diligently studying magic technique. It would be impossible for Sasha to achieve this alone. That meant in the week after learning Gyze, she had practiced Jio Graze and refined it to a level which was usable in battle.

"Are you all ready? Your power, your hearts…entrust them to me."

"Yes, ma'am!"

"We believe in you, Lady Sasha."

"Take all of my power!"

"Let's win this…"

"Let's prove the power of royalty!"

The magic power and determination of twenty people gathered at one central point. This was the true power of Gyze. By using the strengths of each class to one's advantage, group magic with over ten times the power of that of each individual could be activated. When used properly, it could overpower a far superior enemy.

The air was tense.

Then Sasha yelled, "Here goes! *JIO GRAZE!*"

A magic circle like a cannon muzzle appeared at the front of the castle, gathering magic power at its center. Energy accumulated into a great black sun, a comet that was now hurtling in my direction, ready to explode.

Hmm. They'd said they only had a twenty percent chance of success, but this was a perfect Jio Graze.

"Splendid. Allow me to reward you."

I held out my hand towards the incoming Jio Graze. A magic circle appeared, summoning a small flame. Now that I thought about it, this was my first time using attack magic in this era.

"Go."

The flame I'd unleashed collided with the Jio Graze. The next moment, a hole opened in the pitch-black sun, and it was engulfed in its entirety by the flame.

Everything was over in an instant. Jio Graze had burned away without a trace.

"No way… Our Jio Graze was neutralized!"

"L-Lady Sasha! It wasn't just canceled out! His Jio Graze is still…!"

The flame I had released continued on its path towards the castle, where it exploded. The structure was enveloped in fire, crumbling as it burned. The walls and ceilings fell with a loud rumble, collapsing in the blink of an eye.

In the nick of time, Sasha and two of the Mages escaped using Fless. They landed before me on unsteady feet, having consumed the last of their magic.

Sasha groaned as she swayed before me. "To think you could cast Jio Graze all by yourself…"

Hmm. In the Mythical Age, it had been natural to cast Jio Graze by oneself, but there was little point in correcting her. There was something more important to address.

"You should have looked closer at the spell formula. The spell I cast wasn't Jio Graze."

"Huh?" Sasha's eyes rounded in shock. "But there's no higher grade of fire magic than Jio Graze…"

"W-Was it origin magic?!" one of the Mages stammered. "The life-threatening forbidden magic only passed down to royalty would stand a chance of opposing Jio Graze, right?!"

Good grief, they had no understanding at all.

"Sorry to disappoint you, but that wasn't origin magic."

Sasha and her team members stared at me.

"It was Grega."

"What…? G-Grega?"

Fire spells came in different grades. From strongest to weakest, these were: Jio Graze, Griad, Gresde, Gusgam, and Grega.

The Mages began to despair.

"No way… The lowest grade of fire magic swallowed Lady Sasha's Jio Graze and set fire to the castle?!"

"I-Impossible! That can't be! There has to be some kind of trick— some secret to making Grega evolve…"

Of course, there was no secret, so I resolved to enlighten them.

"The only 'secret' is the vast difference in magic power between you and me. Even at twenty against one."

The Mages looked as though they'd been slapped.

"What…"

"Such a thing can't be..."

"It isn't that strange, is it? I'm sure you've seen Gusgam compete with Gresde at some point. When the difference in power is large enough, even Grega can rival Jio Graze."

I took a step forward, causing the Mages to flinch back. They were stricken with despair and had lost all will to fight. Ignoring them, I continued walking over to Sasha.

"Unbelievable... What a monster..." someone muttered behind me.

"Do you recall our wager?" I asked Sasha.

She bit down on her lip, her expression filled with humiliation. "Why didn't you kill me?"

There was no need to get that serious. We weren't at war. This was just a lesson, and it would be a hassle to bring them back to life, but that would hardly be a convincing answer.

"You have potential. It'd be a shame to waste it," I said, offering her my hand. "Become my follower."

Sasha thought for a while, hesitantly reaching for my hand, then glared at me sharply at the last moment. She activated her Magic Eyes and scowled with all her might.

"Die!"

"I refuse," I replied, staring straight into them.

"Then kill me!"

"I refuse." I moved my hand closer towards her. "Stop being so stubborn and join me already."

"I'll never forget this humiliation. One day, I'll be stronger. Then I'll definitely kill you..."

That made me chuckle. "Just know this, Sasha—if I were to die simply from being killed, my existence would have ended two thousand years ago."

Sasha looked dumbfounded. Then, she resigned herself.

"Weird-ass hybrid..." she muttered with a sigh. "Fine. I don't have a hope of winning against you right now, and I can't defy the Zecht." She accepted my offered hand with just the tips of her fingers. "But remember, this is a contract. Don't think you've won over my heart."

"Of course. It's a pleasure to have you on board," I said with a smile.

She blinked in surprise. "Hey. I have one more question."

"What is it?"

"Did you recruit me because of her?"

"Well, yes. Misha looked like she wanted to get along with you."

"I see." She removed her hand with an air of indifference.

"Oh, and one more thing," I added.

"What?"

"Your Magic Eyes were beautiful."

Sasha turned from pink to scarlet. Unsure how else to respond, she turned on her heels as though to run away.

"I'm being sincere, you know. I've never seen such beautiful Eyes before."

Never, even in the Mythical Age, had I seen such pure and tranquil Magic Eyes. If my own Eyes weren't mistaken, she had quite the power hidden within her...though she was lacking much in the way of experience.

"Did you hear me?" I asked, prompting her to turn back towards me.

Embarrassed at my praise, she could only protest weakly. "N-No, you idiot!"

§ 15. The Necron Sisters

Class ended without incident. Unlike the dull theory lessons that had just left me sleepy, the team exam had served as a decent light exercise.

That aside, it had been one week since my acceptance into Delsgade, but I had yet to see a single human invasion, pranking spirit, or scheming god. I'd been on high alert in case I needed to protect Delsgade, but things had been rather anticlimactic. Well, if such weak demons were able to live so prosperously, my strength was probably unneeded.

Who would've thought the land of demons could be so peaceful? Sure, peace was boring, but boring wasn't so bad. It still didn't feel quite real to me, though.

"So, like…" Sasha mumbled beside me as we left the gates of Delsgade. "Why do I have to walk back with you two?"

Misha blinked, tilting her head, so I answered the question for her.

"We're on the same team now, so I figured we could get to know each other."

"I may be your subordinate now, but I never said I'd be your friend."

"Well, you can leave if you want."

"Good. I'm leaving. Goodbye." Sasha spun around and began marching in the opposite direction.

Misha stared wordlessly after her. Although her expression was blank, she seemed sad to see her sister go. I guess there was no helping it.

"You know how I appeared in front of your castle during the exam?"

Sasha froze midstep.

"Do you want me to show you the spell I used?"

Twintails whipped through the air as Sasha turned back around. "I'll hold you to that with *Zecht*."

As expected, she had a keen interest in the topic.

"As you wish."

I signed Sasha's contract. "Here," I said, offering her my hand.

"What...?"

"I said I'd show you. Might as well experience it in person."

"But why do I have to hold your hand?"

"You held it obediently earlier."

Sasha's cheeks flushed red. "Th-That was because of the situation! This is why hybrids are such..." She trailed off, muttering to herself.

"Either way, I can't show you without your hand."

Reluctantly, Sasha obeyed my request.

"Misha."

"Yeah." Misha took my other hand.

"Now you two hold hands as well."

"Huh?! Why should I?" Sasha sure had a varied range of expressions.

"It's against your own contract to refuse to see the spell, you know."

Sasha quieted and held her hand out to Misha. "Fine, here."

Misha hesitantly touched her sister's hand.

"You need to hold on properly," I instructed.

"Like this?" Sasha squeezed my hand.

Misha was also holding firmly to me, but there was only the lightest contact between the two sisters.

"Oh, come on! Hold on to me properly, or the magic won't work," Sasha said, gripping Misha's hand.

"Okay..." Misha squeezed back. Her usually expressionless face was practically beaming with delight.

Good for you, I thought as I watched her, when she looked over at me gratefully. I returned her look with a reassuring smile.

"Hey. If you're gonna talk to each other, say it with your mouths, not your eyes!" Sasha snapped, interrupting us with a glare.

"What? Want to join in?" My eyes met Sasha's, and she looked away, blushing. "Oh, I see. You're not used to making eye contact with people because of your Eyes of Destruction, are you?"

"Wha... That... That's not true..." Her words trailed off till she was inaudible. Bull's-eye. She didn't have control over her Eyes, so it was understandable. If she carelessly made eye contact with someone, she could end up accidentally killing them.

"Enough! Show me the spell already."

"All right, all right. No need to get so noisy."

I cast Gatom. The world around us turned white, and then there we were, standing before a familiar appraisal store and blacksmith's—Wind of the Sun, my home.

"It really is a lost spell... You linked two spaces together, I'm sure of it," Sasha muttered, attempting to analyze the residual magic.

There was no chance of her succeeding, but whatever.

"This is my house. Want to drop by?"

"Forget about that. That spell just now—it was Gatom, wasn't it? Where did a hybrid like you learn the formula for a lost spell? Tell me!" Sasha pressed me for answers, brimming with curiosity.

"If you want to know, you'll have to drop by my house."

"Why would I go into a hybrid's house?"

"There's no need to be shy."

Sasha glared at me, her Eyes lighting in anger. "I'm not!"

"I see, so you're leaving. See you tomorrow, then." I turned my back to Sasha and faced her sister. "You coming in, Misha?"

"Yeah."

"Let's go. We can talk *all* about lost magic today," I said, emphasizing my words as I reached for the doorknob.

"W-Wait a second!"

"Hmm?" I turned around.

"I-Is it..." Sasha mumbled shyly, hanging her head in embarrassment.

"Pardon?"

"Is it okay...if I come too...?"

I chuckled at her meager voice. "Sure."

Sasha sighed in relief.

"So you wanted to hang out after all!"

"No! Listen, my goal is learning about Gatom. *Just* Gatom. I won't stand for any false accusations!"

While that might have been the truth, her flustered denial seemed to admit an ulterior motive. Well, I guessed I could spare her the interrogation—if I upset her into leaving, Misha would be disappointed.

The doorbell rang loudly as I opened the door.

Mom, who had been tending the store, came rushing over. "Welcome home, Anos! How was the exam?" she asked nervously.

"I won."

Mom's face lit up with a sparkling smile as she wrapped me in a tight hug. "That's so amazing, Anos! My darling little genius! Only one month old, yet you're beating all your big friends! That's amazing! Let's celebrate with another feast!"

"Y-Yeah..." As always, mom's enthusiasm knew no bounds. She rubbed her cheek against my own so furiously, even I was at a loss for what to do.

"Oh, mom, I brought another guest over today..."

"Oh? Is it Misha again? Aww, you two are so in love with each other!" Mom swooned, roughly elbowing me in the side. She then turned to Misha, who was standing behind me. "Welcome, Misha! And...?"

Mom looked surprised at the unexpected second guest.

"How do you do, ma'am? My name is Sasha Necron. It's a pleasure to meet you." Sasha lifted the hem of her skirt and curtsied gracefully.

Hmm. How polite of her. Mom was also of mixed blood, but I guess Sasha saw no need to discriminate against those outside of the academy.

"Ma'am? Mom... Mother? You mean..." Mom seemed strangely shocked. "A-Anos... My little Anos has..." She took a deep breath and yelled, "He's brought home a SECOND BRIDE!!!"

Sasha watched in amazement as mom broke down. "Um...what do you mean?"

"Oh, Sasha dear," mom said with a sincere look, grabbing Sasha by the shoulders. "Can you calm down and just listen to me?"

"Don't worry, I'm calm," Sasha replied, implying that mom was the one who needed to calm down.

"Anos is only one month old, so he's still yet to learn the ways of the world," mom cried. "He doesn't have any ill intentions, really! But, you see...he's already made Misha his bride."

For an instant, Sasha was shaken. Then, she coolly said, "Hmm... I see. But that has nothing to do with me."

It was such a calm reply that even mom had to accept it.

"Nothing to do with you...? You mean... You mean you're fine with being a mistress?! Oh, Anos! When did you become so popular?!"

I should have expected no less from mom. Her reputation for unexpected responses was well established.

"Hold on a minute," Sasha interrupted seriously. "That isn't what's happening."

"Huh? Then... Then...are you planning on stealing him?!"

Sasha looked to me for help.

It was funny to watch, so I decided to stay out of it a little longer.

"Um, do you know what Misha's surname is?" Sasha asked my mother.

"Necron, right?"

"Right. And I'm Sasha Necron."

"Oh!" mom gasped. "So…"

"Yes. We're sisters, so I met him by accident—"

"Anos has SISTERS fighting over him! What do I do? What should I do?! Anos's good looks have torn apart the familial bonds of two sisters!"

Just then, the door slammed open, revealing another troublesome relative. It was dad.

"Anos. You know, I was a bit of a bad boy myself back in my youth, using all kinds of swordplay and stuff… Ha ha!"

Hmm. Dad sure wasn't holding anything back either. But why in the world was he talking about his days as a womanizer?

"That's why I know how you feel. Boys will be boys, and I want to be understanding of most things," dad said, deadly serious. "But…two girls at once?! I'm so jealous!"

Father, your true thoughts seem to be showing.

Sasha stared at my family with disapproval, then sighed. "Hey, Anos. Take responsibility."

"With marriage?"

She flushed in an instant. "A-Are you stupid?! That's not what I meant!"

Such a noisy girl.

"Misha! You should speak up too."

Misha thought for a moment. "Do you like Anos, Sasha…?" she then asked.

"You're all *idiots*!"

Hmm. For someone who'd called her a worthless puppet, Sasha sure got along well with Misha.

§ 16. First and Final…

To celebrate my victory in the team exam, mom prepared an extravagant feast.

The dining table was made much livelier by the addition of two people. Most of the noise was coming from my parents, though.

Sasha had mumbled something about not understanding why she had to participate in the celebration of her defeat, but she fell silent the moment she took a bite of mom's cooking. As I'd thought, mom's cooking was delicious even by this era's standards.

"So, how'd it happen?" mom asked Sasha curiously. "What did Anos say when he invited you to his team?"

In the end, dispelling mom's misunderstanding had proven far too difficult. It was now Sasha's turn to be subjected to a barrage of questions, just as Misha had been.

"He didn't say anything special," Sasha replied somewhat stiffly. "'Become my follower,' or something like that."

"Awaaaaaaah! Become my follower? Become my *follower*?! How's a girl supposed to resist such awkward charm?! This lady-killeeerrr!" mom shrieked.

Sasha looked as though she were at a loss for what to do.

"Aaand?" mom pressed. "Why did little Anos want you to join him?"

Sasha's brow twitched. "For no particular reason. Probably because I'm an asset."

"Oho? What was that pause just now? Something's fishy... How did it really go, Misha?"

Misha swallowed her salad before replying. "'Your Magic Eyes were beautiful'...?"

"A... A pickup line like that would make anyone fall head over heels in an instant! Anos is a natural philanderer! The contrast between awkward and smooth is too much, you little charmer!"

Come to think of it, Misha must have heard everything over Leaks. It was standard to cast it alongside Gyze, so I must have used it without thinking.

"Misha, please," Sasha snapped, looking right at her sister. "Can you not say such unnecessary things?"

"Was I not supposed to?" Misha asked, staring back.

Startled, Sasha looked away. "Forget it."

Hmm. She seemed to have surprised herself by speaking directly to Misha while they were supposed to be fighting. Mom, of course, completely misunderstood the exchange and looked between the two of them anxiously. Dad, meanwhile, glanced casually in my direction and gave me a sage nod—as though to say he had nothing more to teach me.

Good grief. After Misha's initial visit, I'd tried to explain that Misha wasn't my betrothed, but mom had sobbed at the thought of us breaking up and wouldn't hear a word of it. Oh well, it was just a harmless misunderstanding. I'd find the right time to clear things up eventually.

And so, the lively dinner came to a close, and it was time for me to see my teammates off. After a quick word with dad in his workshop, I returned to the storefront to find Sasha and Misha waiting for me.

"..."

"..."

The silence was deafening. Misha wasn't very talkative to begin with, but it was unlike Sasha to be so quiet. It sure felt strange seeing her like this. Her talk of Misha being a worthless puppet had made me think they were on bad terms, but she occasionally revealed an attitude that made me think otherwise.

Well, this *was* a world where siblings like Zepes and Leorg existed. I'm sure there were still things I couldn't understand. Misha and Sasha must have their own circumstances.

I decided to give them a little more time together and watched them from the shadows.

The silence continued for over ten minutes. Eventually, Sasha reached her limit and mumbled, "He's late."

"Yeah..."

Again, the silence continued, only to be broken by Sasha.

"Say."

"Hmm?"

"You spoke a lot today."

"Yeah."

"Do you like him?"

"Like him...?"

"Anos, of course."

Misha thought for a moment before responding. "I do."

"I... I see. What's so good about him?"

"He's kind."

"How so? He was evil incarnate in the team exam."

I'd actually been rather benevolent during our bout.

"He's just tough on his enemies..."

"I see. So his behavior is erratic."

The silence resumed.

"What about you, Sasha?"

"What about me?"

"Do you like Anos?"

"Huh?!" Sasha blushed furiously. "As if! That would be absurd."

"I see…"

"That's right."

Misha stared directly at Sasha, whose Eyes triggered from her agitation.

"But…" Sasha mumbled, "he *is* the only one to ever look me in the eye…"

"Yeah…"

"Honestly, it's ridiculous. My Eyes, beautiful? They're cursed to destroy anything they see. Still…" Sasha paused again. "I've never met anyone with the same Eyes before." There was a hint of a smile in her voice. "That's all," she said.

"I see…"

Sasha stared at Misha, who made no attempt to look away.

"Come to think of it, you're the same as him."

"The same…?"

"You can look me in the eye too."

Misha nodded. Her Magic Eyes were also strong—strong enough to resist Sasha's Eyes of Destruction.

"Do you remember how I was shut in a magical cell when we were little? To stop me from destroying everything with my Eyes."

"I remember…"

Sasha looked down as she recalled. "While everyone else was trying to stay out of my sight, you were the only one who kept me company."

"We practiced together."

Sasha smiled at the memory. "We did. Thanks to that, I stopped accidentally hurting people—I just have to avoid their eyes."

"You practiced hard."

Sasha nodded silently. "Say, that thing we did earlier… It brought back memories."

"The thing with our hands…?"

"Yeah."

"It did."

"Can we do it again?" Sasha asked hesitantly.

"Okay."

The two linked hands.

"We used to do this all the time," Sasha continued. "Whenever I cried inside the cell, you'd reach for my hand and smile at me."

Misha nodded.

"Honestly, it'd be hard to tell who's the older one."

"You're the big sister," Misha told her.

Sasha smiled wryly. "Misha, I'm only going to say this once."

Misha nodded.

"I'm sorry. Will you forgive me?"

Misha shook her head. "I was never angry."

Sasha's eyes widened in surprise. "Really?"

"Yeah..."

The two gazed at each other, each squeezing the other's hands.

Hmm. I still had no idea what the circumstances were, but it seemed they'd made up. In fact, they were so close, it was hard to believe they'd been fighting in the first place. Well, they were at that emotional stage of life. Perhaps the fight had been over something petty.

I stepped forward and called out to them. "Sorry for the wait. I'll see you off."

"It's fine. We'll walk back," Sasha said.

I looked over at Misha, who nodded.

"You'd rather spend your time walking? How odd," I commented.

Sasha scowled. "Does it matter? Have a good night."

With their hands linked, the two left my house and set off side by side in silence. I strolled along behind them.

"So why are you following us?" Sasha asked bluntly.

"I said I'd see you off. I always keep my word."

"You were talking about Gatom, though. We're walking."

"It can be pleasant to waste some time occasionally."

The Misfit of Demon King Academy, Vol. 1

"Hmm…" Sasha looked at me as if to say I was strange, but I brushed off her gaze.

In the end, I'd never explained anything about Gatom, and it seemed to have slipped Sasha's mind as well. Mom had probably left too strong of an impression.

"By the way, did you know—"

"Of course," I replied.

Sasha shot me a cold glare with her Magic Eyes. How frightening. If anyone else had been at the receiving end of that look, they'd have been knocked unconscious—if they were lucky.

"I haven't even said anything yet," she said curtly.

"There's nothing I don't know."

"Oh really. Then *I'm sure you know already*, but the Demon King returns this year. That's why the lecturer for our greater magic class tomorrow will be Ivis Necron, one of the Seven Demon Elders."

"Is that so? I didn't know that."

"Then why did you say you did?!"

"Calm yourself. It was a joke."

Seven Demon Elders, huh? That was one of the terms that had been bothering me.

"Sasha. Who exactly are the Seven Demon Elders?"

"I can't believe this. You just said there's nothing you don't know, yet you don't know something so simple? No wonder you're a misfit."

"So, who are they?"

"Two thousand years ago, the founder used his blood to create seven subordinates. These were the first generation descendants of the founder's blood."

"I know that."

I was the founder, after all.

"Then you already know who they are. Those original seven subordinates are the Seven Demon Elders."

"What...?"

Oh, so those guys were the Seven Demon Elders. Come to think of it, I'd created them but had never given them a name. With everything going on with the walls and reincarnation, I hadn't had the time to think about it.

"The Seven Demon Elders trained the first generation of demon lords at Delsgade in preparation for the founder's return."

"I see."

In that case, it should be easy for these Demon Elders to tell I'm the founder. But something was still strange. The current management of Delsgade was far too sloppy for demons of the Mythical Age, and above all, they should know me. So why had I been branded a misfit? I had thought the obsession with one's lineage had caused all this incompetence, but perhaps there was another reason.

I pondered as I walked beside the girls, until...

"Anos...? Hey, Anos!" Sasha called, bringing me back to the present. "What's wrong?"

"Nothing's wrong. We're here. This is our house."

There was a gate in front of us. A grand mansion could be seen past it.

"You've been quiet since I mentioned the Demon Elders. What's up?"

"It's nothing."

"Right. Well, thanks for walking us home. Good night." Sasha turned on her heel and left.

"Bye," Misha added.

"See you tomorrow."

"Yeah." She followed her sister through the gate.

I'd given the misfit thing a lot of thought, but there was still something I was missing. There were several possibilities, but they were all as good as guesses.

Oh well. I'd know more tomorrow after meeting the Demon Elder. There was no need to rush. I had all the time to wait.

For now, it was time to head home. Just as I thought that, Sasha came back out of the gate.

"What's wrong?" I asked her.

"Nothing…"

"Then why did you return?"

"Anos…"

"Hmm?"

Sasha turned her face away, blushing with embarrassment. "Thank you."

"For what?"

"For helping Misha and me make up…"

Ah, so Sasha had wanted to make up too. She was certainly stubborn, to say the least.

"I didn't do much."

"That's not true. No one else would be foolish enough to risk their lives to make *me* their subordinate." She smiled at me. "You're the exception."

Hmm. It hadn't exactly been a life-threatening task for me.

"So, why were you fighting in the first place?"

Sasha frowned. "It was over something stupid. Really stupid… But I just couldn't give in. That's all."

"Has it been resolved?"

"Ah, well…" she mumbled evasively before changing the subject. "I wanted to ask you something."

"Go on."

"If your fate were already decided, what would you do?"

I replied immediately. "If I didn't like it, I'd change it."

She seemed surprised. "You think fate can be changed?"

"Yes, it's simple."

"But how?"

"You crush it with your own hands."

Sasha's eyes widened. Then she giggled. "Hey. Come over here."

"I refuse."

"Wha... Why? Just come over here!"

"I don't like being ordered around."

"Ugh. What an ego." Sasha sighed in exasperation. "Could you please come over here?"

"Better." I walked up to her.

"Closer."

"What are you do—"

As I took another step forward, Sasha's lips pressed against mine.

The kiss caused Leaks to kick in, and I reflexively read her thoughts. It was a kind of curse of mine that was activated under conditions such as this. Sasha's thoughts came flowing into my mind.

This is my first and final kiss.

She bore no ill intent, but I could feel a grim resolution within her. Well, there was no harm in it.

After some time had passed, she abruptly withdrew.

"I-It was just a kiss between friends. As a thank you..." She looked down, cheeks flushed. "Though I haven't done it to anyone else before..."

I wasn't sure what her motives were, but it wasn't my intention to embarrass her.

"I see. Then I've received something quite valuable. Thank you."

Sasha blinked in surprise. "Weird hybrid," she muttered. "I'll see you tomorrow."

"Yeah." I waved my hand, then cast Gatom, but just before my vision turned white—

"Anos... I'm glad I met you..." were the last words to reach my ears.

§ 17. Greater Magic Class

The next day.

I arrived at Delsgade's second lecture hall to find a familiar face to the right of my seat.

"Morning," said Sasha, naturally.

"Wasn't your seat over there?"

"I changed spots. It's better for teams to sit together, no?"

Well, I suppose it did save us the trouble of moving around all the time.

I took my own seat and turned to my left. "Hey."

"Good morning," Misha replied in her usual flat voice.

"Speaking of teams," Sasha said, "what happened to my former teammates?"

"What do you mean?"

"Some of them must have wanted to join your team with me."

Come to think of it, some students had come up to me earlier.

"I rejected them."

"Huh?! Why? Having a bigger team is way better for team exams."

There hadn't been much of a reason for doing so.

"I didn't feel like it," I said.

Sasha was dumbfounded.

"It's not like we need them," I added. "The three of us are enough."

Or rather, *I* was enough.

"We might be fine for the team exams, but you need at least five people to participate in the class ones," she explained. "And you can't join the grade exams with fewer than seven people."

I see, so such rules existed. Even I couldn't win without actually participating.

"I didn't know that."

"So what are we gonna do?"

"There's still time to think. I'll deal with it later."

"What a carefree attitude..." Sasha muttered, scowling.

It was at that moment that the bell rang. Emilia opened the door and stepped inside, followed by a man wearing formal robes and a cap. Perhaps "man" is a little misleading. He was a skeleton. I did recall that one of the seven subordinates I'd created was undead—he must have chosen the name Ivis Necron.

Those with the title Demon Elder must hold considerable power and status in this era. The normally noisy students fell silent the instant Ivis appeared.

Wait. No, this silence was due to the magic he emitted. The overwhelming difference in power between him and the students had them cowering in fright without realizing it.

My own magic should have had a similar effect, but the demons of this era were just too weak to recognize it. Instead of them feeling fear, their senses were completely numbed to my power—they couldn't feel anything at all. Well, if they *could* detect my magic, they would probably drop dead on the spot. That tended to happen to creatures with such low magic resistance. Perhaps this was a survival instinct?

"As I mentioned the other day, today's lesson will be on greater magic," Emilia said, addressing the class. "This lecture, given by the Demon Elder Ivis Necron, will be held only once, so make sure to listen closely." She looked at me as she spoke. "Especially you, Anos Voldigoad. Make sure you're on your best behavior."

All right, but there was no need to call me out like that. I of all people knew how to behave respectfully.

"I know as much without being told," I responded.

"That's good, then..."

Honestly, what was she so worried for? Anyway, this was the perfect opportunity to extend my greeting. I stood up from my seat.

"Yo, Ivis. Long time no see."

Emilia's jaw dropped to the floor. "A-A-Anos Voldigoad! H-How dare you address Lord Ivis that way?!"

The students began whispering amongst themselves.

"He's dead... He's dead for sure this time."

"Yeah, acting like that with a Demon Elder is going too far..."

"Wait, won't we be collateral damage if he makes Lord Ivis mad?"

"Give us a break, misfit..."

Ignoring the din, I used my Eyes to check out Ivis. His magic was familiar, meaning he was indeed one of the subordinates I'd created using my blood. I was almost certain of it—*almost.*

"Lord Ivis, please accept my sincerest apologies!" Emilia pleaded. "I shall have Anos Voldigoad expelled immediately!"

"No need," said Ivis cordially. His voice emanated from the eerie jawbone ornament that hung over his chest. "You say you've seen me before."

He turned to look at me. The students ducked under their desks, scurrying to activate anti-magic barriers. What were they so afraid of?

"Yeah, it's been two thousand years. Don't you remember?"

"Two thousand years," Ivis murmured, nodding. "No wonder. Unfortunately, I have no memories of that time. I only remember my master, the Demon King of Tyranny."

"Then you should remember me."

"Are you connected to the founder?"

Hmm. So that's how it was. Ivis remembered the Demon King of Tyranny but had no idea who I was. In other words, he believed someone else was the Demon King. Perhaps his memory loss had something to do with it, but something was still rather off. The Seven Demon Elders were the heads of the academy. Even if Ivis had lost his memory, it was impossible for the other six to have lost theirs at the same time. Not by coincidence, anyway. Had someone altered their memories? Or was he feigning his memory loss?

"Your magic does feel somewhat familiar," Ivis admitted.

"Is that so?"

"Yes. I'm sure we were acquainted."

Either way, conversing wouldn't give me answers.

"What did you want from me?" he asked.

"Oh, nothing in particular. I just figured I could help jog your memory."

Under the worried gaze of the rest of the class, I marched up to Ivis. Then, a foot before him, I seized his skull with an eagle grip.

The classroom was overrun with panic.

"Wh-What are you doing, Anos?!" Emilia cried.

"He's done it now! He's really gone and done it!"

As the students behind me broke into a clamor, I drew a magic circle on my palm.

"Remember. Remember the name of your master: Anos Voldigoad."

The magic I'd activated was Eviy, a spell that could evoke memories, even of the distant past, but there was no response from Ivis's mind.

"Your efforts are futile," Ivis said. "No memory remains of that time. It's not that I cannot remember. The memories do not exist. Not even Eviy can bring back what is lost."

"How about this, then?" I layered my magic circle, deploying Rivide, an origin spell, over Eviy.

"What is this...? What have you done? My memories... They're flowing into my mind..."

"If your memories have been erased, I'll simply rewind time within your mind with Rivide and activate Eviy to retrieve them from two thousand years ago."

"Rewind time? Impossible! Are you saying there's magic that can transcend time?!"

"It's a type of origin magic. A rather difficult spell to cast, though."

By using Demon King Anos and the memory of Ivis of two thousand years ago as an origin, I could cast Rivide to reverse time, rewinding it to the point of origin. Two thousand years of memories were flashing before Ivis's eyes.

He looked thoughtful. "Indeed, I've recalled the last two millennia..."

...But there was nothing there. There wasn't a single mention of the Demon King Anos Voldigoad in two thousand years of memories.

Of course, the memories were flowing into Ivis's head, not my own, so I could only see the surface of them, but that was enough to make out the names mentioned within them. Mine was nowhere to be found. Instead, the name that repeatedly appeared was that of the Demon King of Tyranny Avos Dilhevia.

"Why do I still have no memory of you?"

"Someone has completely wiped your memories of the last two thousand years. There's no telling at what point it happened."

Put simply, his past had been altered. To him, the Demon King Anos had never existed to begin with. Someone had tampered with his mind using magic.

How troublesome. No matter how far back I went with Rivide, there was no way for me to retrieve his past—it had ceased to exist. Ivis's memories, too, were lost to the void of time.

"I see. Anos, was it? I must thank you. That fact alone is new knowledge to me. It means there's someone out there who wishes me ill."

Was he being serious or just playing the fool? It was also possible that he'd altered his past himself to escape my notice.

"Don't mention it. Please get on with the lesson."

My classmates whispered frantically as I returned to my seat.

"What just happened?!"

"I have no idea! I thought he was done for, but now he's being thanked?!"

"Why would an Elder thank someone for grabbing him?!"

"What does this even mean?!"

"He was thanked by a Demon Elder... That's insane!"

"Is he really a misfit...?"

"Whoa! I don't get what happened, but wow!"

I pulled out my chair and sat down.

Misha turned to me. "I'm glad you're safe..."

"I can't believe you sometimes," Sasha muttered from my other side.

This class sure liked to make a huge fuss over nothing.

But Avos Dilhevia, huh? I'd thought my name had been corrupted over the passage of time, but that no longer seemed to be the case. The Seven Demon Elders, the Demon King Academy, and my brand as a misfit... I couldn't say for sure, but all of it may have been calculated.

This Avos Dilhevia was trying to replace me.

§ 18. The Secret Art of Necron

Unaffected by the earlier fuss, Ivis began the lesson.

"Today's lecture will be on fusion magic, the secret art of the Necron family."

He drew the basic formula for fusion magic on the blackboard. It was a natural magic circle that used moonlight as its base. The gates and runes were very similar to those used in the Mythical Age. It was a rather complex spell formula. The students were struggling to copy it down, but it was no problem for me.

So this was what magic that had been researched since the Mythical Age looked like. It was a fascinating sight. If my regular classes were more like this, perhaps I wouldn't get so sleepy.

"Hey, Anos, shouldn't you be taking notes or saving this to a recording crystal?" Sasha asked in a hushed voice.

"I have a record of it already—in here," I said, tapping my temple.

"You've got to be kidding me..." she muttered. "You memorized such a complex formula just by looking at it?"

"I don't see you taking any notes either."

"It's the secret art of the Necron family. I'm a direct descendant, so I mastered the basics years ago."

Oh, that's right.

"Since you're a direct descendant, does that make you close with Ivis?"

"No way. The Seven Demon Elders are way higher in status. I may be a direct descendant, but I'm sixteenth in line—the very lowest. I've only ever spoken to Lord Ivis once…"

Demons have substantial life spans. It made sense for so many of Sasha's forebears to still be alive.

"As I explained just now," Ivis continued, "the greatest advantage of fusion magic comes from the fusion of two sources of power. The union of two distinct wavelengths of magic induces a powerful magic reaction that can increase the base power more than tenfold. This is the lowest grade of fusion magic, Je Gum."

Sasha leaned closer. "Say…are you really memorizing all this? You're not just saying that, right?"

"Skeptic much?"

"It took me a whole month to understand this spell…"

"What's so strange about that? It's only natural for something that takes *you* a month to take *me* a second."

Sasha glared daggers at me. She seemed discontent at the idea of me being a faster learner. The Magic Eyes of Destruction flickered in her pupils.

"Shall I prove it to you?" I offered.

"How so?"

Ivis had just wrapped up a section of his lecture. "Are there any questions?"

A nervous air flooded the classroom. Not a single student was brave enough to raise their hand.

"May I?" I asked, breaking the silence.

"Go ahead."

As I stood up, the students began whispering.

"What's he going to say this time?"

"I can't believe he has the guts to put his hand up before a Demon Elder."

"Totally. He must have nerves of steel..."

"If he says something stupid, he could be killed."

Good grief. It was hard to believe such timid demons were my own flesh and blood.

"There's a flaw in the structure of that circle—in fact, the basic fusion formula itself is fatally flawed."

The classroom fell deathly silent. Had my words frozen the room?

"Oh no... He's done it now. It's over for real this time. This isn't the same as talking back to Ms. Emilia!"

"Saying there's a flaw in the secret art of Necron is the same as saying a Demon Elder's wrong. He's crazy..."

"There's no way a formula developed by an Elder could be flawed in the first place!"

In contrast to the noise of the students, Ivis's voice was calm.

"A flaw?"

"This basic formula can indeed be used to fuse magic power. It is also capable of increasing the base power as you say. However, the fusion won't last for very long with this structure."

The students braced themselves with magic barriers and anti-magic spells as though Ivis would destroy the classroom at any moment.

"I'm impressed," Ivis acknowledged. "It's quite the feat to notice that at first glance."

The class was taken aback.

"I-Impressed...?!"

"Did he mean to say incensed?"

"Glance?!"

"Calm down, man. 'Glance' is a perfectly normal word..."

Ivis added notes about fusion duration to the blackboard. "The fusion duration is indeed regrettably short. This is due to the structure of the basic spell formula, so no matter the grade of spell used, the flaw cannot be eliminated."

"The average caster can only maintain a fusion duration of three to five seconds," I added. "With a formula as complex as this, the magic is hardly worth using."

Ivis nodded in agreement. "There are indeed limits to the use of fusion magic. In almost all cases, it would be better to substitute it. However, if you look deeper into the abyss, you'll see that this magic has immense potential."

Heh. As expected of a subordinate born from my blood. Although he couldn't complete the formula himself, his Eyes had a clear view of his goal.

"I agree. When I looked into the abyss, I saw the true base formula for fusion magic."

Even Ivis was surprised. His magic power trembled.

Notebook pages fluttered, and pens clattered to the ground.

"Aaahhh! It's over... We're dead. Deeead!"

"N-No! I don't want to die yet! Why did I have to be in the same class as the misfit?!"

My classmates shook in their seats, preparing themselves for their deaths.

"You say you can improve this formula?" came the low voice, tinged with faint bewilderment.

"With ease."

"I've devoted over a thousand years to this spell..."

"Just watch." I left my seat.

"Hey..." Sasha hurriedly interrupted, trying her best to stop me. "Fusion magic is the secret of the Necron family! You may have seen Gyze before, but this is—"

"It's just a lesson; what are you so worried about?"

Pouting, Sasha turned swiftly away. "I-It's not that I'm worried or anything..."

"Watch this." I walked up to the blackboard and used my magic to redraw the formula. "How's that?" I then asked, turning to Ivis.

The moment Ivis saw it, he gulped. Moments later, he began to shiver. The formula drawn on the blackboard had power flowing through it. Truly understanding the structure required good Eyes and substantial knowledge, but it was clear from a single glance that the formula was valid.

"What... What is this?" Ivis stammered, frantically analyzing the spell. "The fusion duration has increased several hundredfold... I see you've incorporated origin magic into the formula, but how did you integrate the two?"

"It's simple. I used the fusion spell itself to fuse the two formulae together."

"What?!" Ivis was speechless. I guess the thought had never occurred to him.

There are some things that are looked at by many but are only truly seen by few. Once the solution was pointed out, it was obvious the answer had been right there all along. That was the essence of magic research.

"Such an extraordinary idea... Anos Voldigoad, was it? I never imagined someone would have researched fusion magic before me."

"Ah, I see." There was a little misunderstanding I had to correct. "Ivis. This work belongs to you."

"What...?"

"Today was my first time seeing this formula. Without your research, I couldn't have completed it. All I did was give it the final push."

Ivis was astounded. "How...? It was your first time seeing the formula, yet you understood it and perfected it in a matter of moments!"

"You would have figured it out yourself given another thousand years."

Having proven my point, I returned to my seat.

"Why is a monster like you attending the academy?" he murmured. "There's nothing I can teach you, Anos Voldigoad..."

Once again, the class erupted into chaos.

"What just happened?"

"We're alive!"

"I know we're alive! But...what?!"

"I... I don't get it, but I think Anos perfected the formula for fusion magic!"

"What's up with him...? Is he really a misfit?!"

"Does 'misfit' actually mean 'genius'?"

"Hey, you're so shocked you've forgotten what words mean again!"

When I reached my seat and sat back down, I looked over at Sasha, whose jaw was still hanging open.

"See? I told you I understand it."

"I don't even know what to say anymore..."

§ 19. Dungeon Exam

During the lunch break after greater magic class, I stood in the hallway talking to Ivis.

"So you mean to say you're my master, the Demon King of Tyranny?"

"Yes, the Demon King's true name is Anos Voldigoad. Someone's rewritten history and changed that name to Avos Dilhevia."

Ivis listened with an open mind. "Who would do such a thing?"

"I don't know yet, but it's probably the same person who erased your memories."

"I see," Ivis said, thoughtfully bringing a hand to his jawbone. "That would indeed explain my lack of memories. However, Anos, it is also possible that *you* were responsible for erasing my memories."

He shot me a penetrating look with his Magic Eyes.

"Unfortunately, I have no proof of my innocence."

"You possess immense talent. I cannot overlook the risk you may pose to the Demon King of Tyranny."

Ivis was no fool. With no memories, he had no means of discerning whether I was the real deal. In such a case, it was only natural to consider the possibility I was the enemy. As far as he knew, I was the only one who could use Rivide. That meant I was perfectly capable of erasing two thousand years of memories myself. It wouldn't be strange for him to suspect me of pretending to be an ally while aiming to overthrow the Demon King.

"I shall remain neutral for now. There's something about you that feels familiar."

"I'd appreciate it."

"Farewell."

Ivis left, watched by the surrounding students.

"That was Demon Elder Ivis Necron just now, right...?"

"It was... Lord Ivis never even speaks to black-uniform students, so why was he with that kid in white?"

"Hey, could that be the rumored misfit everyone's talking about?"

"What business would a misfit have with a Demon Elder?"

Students from other classes, huh? This school sure loved its gossip. Was there really a need to concern oneself with others?

"Anos."

I turned at the sound of my name to see Emilia approaching.

"This was left behind," she said, handing me a badge. On it was a six-pointed star. It wasn't mine. "Please give it to its rightful owner."

"Whose is this?"

"It belongs to a member of your team."

So either Sasha or Misha. I hadn't taken a close enough look at either of their insignias to know which, though.

"Which one?"

Emilia shifted in discomfort. "The one who isn't Sasha."

What an odd way of phrasing it. She could have just said Misha.

"Isn't it a bit negligent to use me as an errand boy? You could give it to her yourself."

I thought Emilia would be offended by my response, but she simply looked troubled. Well, whatever. Misha must be looking for it.

"I'll make sure it gets to her." I turned to walk away when Emilia called out to me.

"There's a dungeon exam this afternoon, so come to the dungeon entrance instead of the classroom."

"All right."

I left the hallway, following Misha's magic to the courtyard. A crowd had formed with Sasha and Misha at its center.

"Look, there's nothing I can do. If you want to join the team, you have to speak to Anos."

"But, Lady Sasha, that misfit has no intention of hearing us out. If you could put in a word for us..."

"In that case, give up. There's nothing I can say that will convince him."

Sasha's former team members, huh? It seemed like they wanted to join my team to be with her. That was some pretty desperate pleading.

Misha was beside them, but no one bothered to ask her. If they wanted to join me, she was just as capable of putting in a word. It would also make more sense to ask her, since she had been on my team from the beginning, while Sasha had only joined recently. Did they ignore her because she was wearing a white uniform? Or because they didn't know her well enough to ask for favors?

Come to think of it, I'd never seen Misha speak to another demon before. Well, she didn't have the disposition to talk to others first—I was usually the one to initiate conversations between us.

"Lady Sasha, are you truly content with being on that misfit's team? Or is there another reason behind this?"

Sasha frowned in annoyance. "I have no choice but to obey the contract. Besides, if you want to look down on Anos, you can do so *after* you've perfected fusion magic."

The students fell silent. There was nothing they could say to that.

"Are you done now? Then go." Sasha sighed to herself as the group reluctantly dispersed.

"What a refreshing rejection to listen to," I observed. "Fitting for a subordinate of mine."

Sasha's eyes widened, and she turned away in a huff. It seemed she hadn't realized I was there. "Shut up. They were just being annoying," she muttered.

"Misha, you dropped this," I said, holding out the insignia.

"Thank you." Misha took the badge and attached it to her uniform. "Did you come to get us?" she asked.

"For what?"

"The dungeon exam this afternoon."

Ah right, that. Put simply, we had to venture into the labyrinth far below Delsgade. We would be separated into the same teams as before to compete over the magic items, weapons, and armor left in the dungeon. The lengthier explanation involved something about training us in the techniques required to navigate a labyrinth, but it was really nothing more than a treasure hunt.

"That wasn't my intention, but I guess I'm right on time."

"Yeah."

We were to meet in front of the dungeon entrance and so had to get moving a little earlier.

"Speaking of which, Anos, were you listening to the instructions?"

"Yes. The team that nabs the scepter from the altar on the lowest floor gets full marks. Easy."

"You weren't listening at all! It's impossible to get full marks in this exam. Not even the teachers have reached the lowest floor, much less a student. They're not even sure if the scepter actually exists—or the lowest floor itself!"

"Then why is it included in the specifications?"

"I don't know… Maybe because there's a legend about it?"

Good grief, why was this school so sloppy with things like this?

"The scepter is the one said to amplify the power of Gyze, right?"

"Yes. They say the founder himself created it."

"In that case, it exists. Assuming no one else has taken it, that is."

Sasha sighed. "There you go speaking nonsense again… Well, whatever. Let's get going. It's almost time."

As we walked, Misha looked up at me. "How do you know it exists…?"

"It's my castle."

She tilted her head.

We continued towards the entrance to the underground. It'd been a long time since my last trip down there. When we arrived, we found the rest of class two already gathered there. Just as we got into position, the bell rang, and Emilia began to address us.

"The dungeon exam will now commence. Any items obtained by team members within the dungeon are property of the team leader. You have until nine o'clock tomorrow morning. Students who return early may go home as they please. Anyone who wishes to give up may contact me using Leaks." She opened the door to the dungeon. "May the founder bless you."

At the signal, the students charged inside. I walked leisurely behind them.

"Hey, Anos?" Sasha called. "We're gonna fall behind. It's first come first served, so we can't be walking so slowly!"

"It's fine," I assured her.

"Fine?"

"You can go on ahead if you want."

"There's no point in me going alone."

Sasha turned away angrily, marching along a few steps ahead of us. There were monsters positioned throughout the dungeon for the exam, but the students that had gone first had defeated them all, allowing us to proceed unchallenged.

"Take a right there," I ordered.

"How do you know which way to go?"

"I've been here before."

Sasha looked skeptical but continued reluctantly in the direction I pointed. We proceeded as such and had descended ten floors or so when Misha turned to me.

"Can I ask something?"

"What is it?"

Misha looked over at Sasha, who was still walking ahead of us. "What would be a good birthday present?"

"For Sasha?"

She nodded. "It's tomorrow…"

I see. This was short notice. Well, I guess it couldn't be helped since they'd only made up yesterday.

"Sasha," I called after her.

"What?"

"Is there anything you want right now?"

"To get the top mark in this exam, of course."

What an uninspiring answer.

"There you have it," I told Misha.

"That's a problem…"

"It's something you can definitely give her."

Misha shook her head. "I want it to be something she'll always remember."

That raised the bar much higher.

"I'm sure she'd be happy with anything as long as it's from you."

"Really…?"

"She was smiling when the two of you made up."

Misha pondered vacantly for a moment. "Clothes would be nice."

Clothes, huh? Perhaps a certain item in the deepest vault would be sufficient.

"I know of something she might like, then."

"Oh?"

"It just so happens to be down below. If we find it, it's yours."

Misha offered me a rare smile. "Thank you."

"When's your birthday, by the way?"

"Also tomorrow."

Oh, so they were twins. No wonder they looked so alike.

"Is there anything you want?"

Misha thought for a moment. "There's nothing…"

"No need to be reserved."

"But I won't see you tomorrow…"

Even if we weren't planning on seeing each other, I could give her a birthday present at any time, no? Or was it true there was nothing she wanted? Well, I could just force her to accept it.

"How old will you be?"

"Fifteen."

So Sasha must be turning the same. The two had been born fifteen years prior to the year the Demon King was said to reincarnate. Despite this gap, Sasha was rumored to be the reincarnation of the founder. It seemed the dominant belief was that the founder would be reincarnated into an existing vessel of power rather than as a newborn baby. Or that I would awaken several years after reincarnating.

I hadn't specified how I would reincarnate, so it was possible that true events differed from legend. If I thought about it that way, it was also possible that the Demon King Academy was designed so as not to recognize a newborn, preventing me from being recognized as the founder.

"Anos?" Sasha called, turning to me after reaching the end of the corridor. "This is a dead end."

"No, there's a hidden passage."

"There can't be. I checked with my Eyes, but there's nothing."

"There are countermeasures in place to protect against Magic Eyes," I said, walking straight to the end of the corridor.

"Huh? Wait, Anos, what—"

I headbutted the wall, smashing right through it. The wall crumbled, creating a hole the shape of my body as I continued to pass through with brute force.

"Huuuh?!" Sasha cried.

"He's sturdy…" Misha added.

"Sure, he's stupidly sturdy…but can you really call that a hidden passage?"

"I couldn't tell with my Eyes…"

"Well yeah, there wasn't anything magical about it."

Sasha and Misha stared after me, completely stunned.

"Come on," I said.

With a bewildered expression, Sasha began walking. "He just broke through the wall…"

"Yeah…" Misha replied.

§ 20. Demon Castle Vault

After breaking enough of the wall by walking through it, we arrived at a spacious room. It was a hidden chamber that led to the lowest floor of the dungeon.

Sasha looked surprised. "There's a room on the other side..."

"Passages hidden with magic are surprisingly easy to spot. All you have to do is follow the traces of magic power. Regular hidden passages are actually harder to notice."

The only downside was having to fix the holes with Iris every time one passed through.

"But the dungeon below Delsgade is normally off-limits to students," Sasha said doubtingly. "How did you know this would be here?"

"What if I told you I built it?"

She pouted unhappily. "Fine, don't answer."

It was actually the truth, but alas.

"Let's go. This room leads to the bottom floor."

We walked for a short while until we reached another room, this one illuminated by natural light. The ceiling loomed high above us, and despite being so far underground, the room was brimming with lush greenery. A waterway ran through the landscape, its surface glinting in the light.

"Sunlight…" Misha murmured.

"That's right. It was designed to let in sunlight during the day and moonlight at night."

"To activate natural magic circles?"

The Necron family's secret art of fusion magic used natural circles. Both Misha and Sasha's familiarity with the topic allowed them to identify the room at a glance—a room that acted as a catalyst for magic.

However, things were a little different from how I remembered them from two thousand years ago. The sunlight was flowing in at a different angle. Had someone adjusted the environment for a spell? The dungeon had been used not only by me, but also by my subordinates, so it wouldn't be that unusual.

I looked up at the ceiling. It was a completely normal ceiling—there was nothing out of the ordinary to be seen.

"Is something wrong…?" Misha asked.

"No, it was just my imagination."

We proceeded forward, leaving the natural circle room. After what seemed like an eternity of descending a staircase, Sasha turned to me.

"Say, Anos, if you've been here before, can't you use Gatom to get here?"

"The anti-magic cast on the dungeon interferes with Gatom. You can use it, but there's no telling where you'll end up."

It was easy to remove the anti-magic, but the dungeon was designed to self-destruct if one did so. If I'd made it so that only I was able to use Gatom, it would have been the same as creating a loophole. The surest way of preventing intruders was to make it so that even I couldn't use Gatom.

"We've been walking for two hours already," Sasha whined. "How much farther is it?"

"Look." Misha pointed ahead. We could see the end of the staircase.

"We're here. This is the bottom floor."

"Really?" Sasha ran down the last few steps ahead of us, but when she saw what was before her, she came to a dazed stop.

Misha and I caught up. Sasha had stopped before a majestic door, large enough to accommodate a giant.

"This is the door to the altar room."

Misha activated her Magic Eyes and stared at the door. "Anti-magic."

"Yep. To stop anyone from magically destroying the door."

Misha stared deeper into the abyss. "Not even Jio Graze can destroy it…"

"Huh?! Then how do we get inside?" exclaimed Sasha. It seemed she was still unaware of her company.

"Try using your head," I told her. "If you only focus on destroying it, you'll come to a dead end. Think about it. If magic doesn't work, you can just open it without magic."

I stepped forward, placing my hand on the door. Then, with a hard push, the heavy door creaked open. "See? It's open."

Sasha stared at me, astonished. "First you lift an entire castle, and now this… What is your body made of? How can you open such a stupidly large door?"

She tried pushing it herself, but naturally, it didn't budge. Nice try.

"It's thanks to my daily training regimen."

"This is way beyond the level you get to simply by working out. Was there ever a bloodline with this much strength…?" Sasha trailed off, muttering to herself.

"More importantly, our goal is right over there," I said, setting us back on track. A sinister-looking staff rested against the altar at the back of the room.

"That's…the scepter, right?"

If Sasha looked with her Magic Eyes, she would instantly see the tremendous amount of power residing within the stick. It was worlds apart from Zepes's matchstick of a demon sword—this was a genuine product of the Mythical Age.

"Now we're guaranteed full marks."

I'd almost expected someone to have taken it, so I was glad to see it was still here.

"Say…can I touch it?"

Items acquired in the dungeon exam were considered property of the team leader. However, a magic item of this caliber had been a rare find even in the Mythical Age. It was only natural for someone with such sharp Magic Eyes to express an interest.

"Go ahead."

"Thanks!"

She rushed eagerly to the altar, picking up the scepter. Her Eyes were captivated by the ancient mystery of the staff, so much so that she stared at it, unmoving.

Hmm. Perfect timing. She'd be immersed in it for a while.

"Misha, this way," I said, heading towards one of the doors in the altar room.

"What is it…?"

"The treasure vault."

We entered the vault. At first glance, it was entirely empty. However, one simply had to utter the words "reveal thyself" to lift the magic veil and uncover all kinds of demon swords, enchanted armor, and accessories. All were items I had gathered in the Mythical Age.

Amongst them were numerous dazzling garments such as the Moonwoven Dress, crafted from refined moonlight and rare magic threads harvested from the Spellstrand Dragon, or the Golden Lion Robe, woven from the fur of the Golden Lion said to be the most beautiful creature in the world.

"Pick one that suits Sasha."

Misha stared with Magic Eyes at one of the garments in the vault. Good choice. She wasn't looking at the appearance of the clothes, but at the abyss behind them.

The magic items of the Mythical Age chose their owners. It was one thing for the owner to use the item, but gifting one to another wasn't so simple. Now, how would this go?

After a while, Misha walked forward. "This one."

The present she'd picked was the Phoenix Mantle, fabricated from the plumage of the divine bird. It granted its wearer the blessing of eternal fire—at the risk of burning away whomever it deemed unworthy of wearing it, that is.

"I know it looks pretty, but it won't be easy to wear," I warned.

"Yeah," she replied.

It seemed she understood that. Misha had good enough Eyes to see that Sasha would be worthy of the garment.

"Then go and give it to her."

Misha smiled, carefully taking the Phoenix Mantle in both hands and starting for the door back to the altar room. She paused, however, as her gaze wandered across the vault. A ring displayed on a pedestal had caught her eye.

It was the Lotus Ice Ring, a ring cold enough to blanket the seven seas with ice sheets the shape of lotus leaves. And it was no coincidence that she'd spotted it—magic items and their owners were naturally drawn to one another. In this case, the Lotus Ice Ring was calling out to her.

"Do you want it?"

Misha remained expressionless and continued staring at the ring.

"It's also your birthday tomorrow."

She shook her head. "It's okay," she told me, rushing out of the treasure vault as if running away.

"Hmm."

Perhaps there were certain circumstances preventing her from being honest. I pocketed the Lotus Ice Ring and followed her out of the vault.

"Ahah!" Sasha cried, scurrying up to us with the scepter in her hands. "Where did you two go? You were gone when I turned around, so I was getting worried."

"Apologies," I said, smiling slightly. "Were you lonely?"

"I said I was *worried!*"

What was there to be shy about? If she'd felt uneasy being alone, she should just say so.

"Stop looking at me like that," she snapped. "It feels so arrogant."

"Looking at you like what? The word arrogant doesn't exist in my dictionary."

"You can look in the mirror for the definition."

She sure liked to spout nonsense.

"By the way, are we done here?" she asked, turning back to the altar.

All that was left of the dungeon exam was to return to the entrance, but there was one more thing we could get done while here.

"Why don't you give that to her?" I asked Misha, who was hiding behind my back.

"Now...?"

"Were you going to hide it the whole way back?"

Misha thought for a moment, then shook her head and stepped out. "Sasha."

Sasha looked at her. When she saw the Phoenix Mantle in Misha's hands, her eyes widened. "What's that you have there, Misha?"

"I found it..."

"Here?"

Misha nodded. "I'm giving it to you."

"What... To me? Are you sure? This is one hell of an item..." Sasha must have noticed the tremendous power hidden within the robe. She stared at it closely.

"It's your birthday tomorrow."

At those words, Sasha smiled softly. Stray tears gathered at the corners of her eyes. "But I didn't get you anything..."

"There's nothing I need."

Sasha gave her a troubled smile. "Thank you, Misha. I love it. I'll treasure it forever."

Misha smiled back. "Yeah..."

Magic circles glimmered in Sasha's eyes as she gazed at the Phoenix Mantle. It was her Magic Eyes of Destruction—there was no reason for her to use them here, so it was probably an uncontrollable reaction in response to her heightened emotions.

But something was strange. If she was overjoyed at receiving the gift, the magic circles should have appeared as soon as her birthday was mentioned. Had she recalled something that had made her emotions rise while she stared at the robes? What could it be?

"Can I try it on?"

Misha nodded, handing the robes to her sister.

Sasha reached for the top button of her blouse, then gasped and whipped around towards me. "I'd like to change..."

"Ah. I'll turn around then."

"That's not good enough! Go wait inside that room!"

Honestly, how troublesome could one be? There was no helping it. I did as she'd ordered and headed back into the vault.

Just as I was about to close the door, Misha peeked around the corner.

"She liked it..."

"That's great."

"It's all thanks to you."

"You're the one who chose it."

Misha blushed. "Today is the best day of my life..."

"That's quite the statement."

She shook her head. "Thank you."

I nodded, closing the door behind me.

§ 21. Sasha's True Intentions

I leaned against the wall of the treasure vault, gazing vacantly into space. They sure were taking a while... Ten minutes had already passed. How long did it take to change into a robe? I knocked on the door to prompt them to hurry, but there was no response from the other side.

"How strange."

Sasha may not have answered, but Misha would certainly have opened the door as soon as I knocked. They wouldn't have left without me, would they? Unless...

"Misha, are you there? I'm opening the door."

There was no response, so I opened it. From there, I looked over at the altar. There was something distinctly different about it.

It was red.

Blood pooled at its base, where Misha was slumped over on her knees. A knife protruded from the right side of her chest. It looked like she was still alive, but a magic barrier had been carefully erected to prevent her from being healed.

"Oh? So you've finally come to join us. You were awfully obedient." Sasha's voice rose from the opposite side of the room from the altar. She wore the Phoenix Mantle and grasped the scepter in one hand.

"What is the meaning of this, Sasha?"

She sneered. "Ha! Dumbass. You were completely fooled by the nice-girl act. Did you really think I'd get along with a worthless doll like her? It was all part of my plan to get first place in the dungeon exam."

An act, huh? So her efforts to make up with Misha, her happiness when they'd made up, and the tears she'd shed over her birthday present had all been lies?

"Men are such simple creatures. One little kiss and they fall into the palm of your hand. Did you really believe I'd fall for a half-breed like you?"

"That was quite the performance, Sasha," I said.

Sasha faltered, then glared at me. "What's that supposed to mean...?"

"I just didn't peg you for the acting type."

"Right. It was a fine performance, wasn't it?"

"It was far too lax for a betrayal scene. If you want to do it properly, you should kill Misha, cut up her body to prevent her resurrection, seal her flesh in stones, then hide those stones across the world. And that's just the start. Why didn't you do that?"

Sasha frowned. She seemed rather disgusted by the suggestion, which only proved she wasn't suited for cruelty.

"All you've done is stroke her chest with a knife. What are you playing at?"

"Shut up. My only goal was to come first in the exam."

That didn't add up either.

"Even if the scepter's in your hands, you're still a member of my team."

Items obtained in the dungeon were property of the team leader. Nonetheless, Sasha grinned and activated a magic circle.

"I'm breaking our *Zecht*."

As she spoke the word, the contract between Misha and Sasha

dissipated. Without it, our agreement was annulled, allowing her to leave my team whenever.

However, Misha hadn't agreed to breaking the Zecht. The principles of Zecht made it impossible to break without the agreement of both parties. Even in death, the effect of the spell continued.

It was hard to imagine Sasha having enough power to break a Zecht with brute force. There were several alternate possibilities that came to mind, but one stood out as the most reasonable.

"I see. How fascinating," I murmured in response.

Sasha, who'd thought herself in the superior position, for some reason looked panicked. "Are you out of your mind? She's going to die if you leave her like that. Should you really be acting so carefree in a situation like this?"

"What situation would that be? From where I stand, this is no more than another boring afternoon lesson," I said. Sasha's gaze grew increasingly harsher. "A lesson during which the sisterly bickering has gotten a little out of hand, I suppose."

"I told you I've never thought of that piece of trash as my sister!" she yelled angrily. "Listen here. That *thing* was born to be used by me. A dirty rag to be disposed of after serving its purpose. She's nothing more than a pathetic, miserable magic doll."

She spat out her words with disgust. "Aha ha! Aha ha ha ha! I can't believe she actually forgave me. How many times will she fall for the same thing? Such a stupid doll who never learns. Did she really think we could get along? At least she was good for one thing. She helped me fool this stupid hybrid. Isn't that great?"

She turned to Misha. "Hey, Misha, are you still alive? There's one last thing I wanted to say to you. I've always hated it—I hated the way you acted all innocent and naive, believing in me no matter how many times I deceived you!"

Sasha's emotions peaked with the rise in her voice, yet there was no sign of the Magic Eyes of Destruction in her pupils. They hadn't shown up at any point during her speech.

"And?" I asked, taking a step forward. "What about how you really feel?"

She glared at me, her Magic Eyes finally flaring up.

"What? Are you mad that I saw right through you?"

Sasha's glare gave way to a huff of laughter. "Oh? Did you really believe I can't control my Magic Eyes?" She smiled and closed her eyes. When she slowly opened them again, the magic circles were gone. "See? I'm in total control."

The somewhat relieved look on her face made her claim hard to believe.

"So you're saying I'm mistaken. I see. So, tell me—" I took another step forward "—what's really going on?"

Sasha bit down on her lip. Was she wary of my approach, or was she...

"You're just the same as that doll, aren't you? I heard about what happened with Zepes and Leorg—expecting siblings to get along and all that garbage. Not all of us are carefree, naive idiots that only know a peaceful world, you know?"

So now I was naive? Sure, I didn't know much about the current world, but to say I only knew a peaceful one was laughable.

"Just because you have a little power doesn't mean you can say what you want!" she continued. "Stop trying to be the good guy when you don't know anything!"

"I refuse."

My reply left Sasha speechless.

"I'll say what I want to say, when I want to say it. I'll listen to what I want to listen to, when I feel like listening. I don't take orders from anyone."

Of course, I normally minded my manners, but there was no need to hold back now.

"Sasha, I truly hope you didn't believe I'd allow one of my subordinates to lay their hands on a friend."

I walked towards Sasha, who tightened her grip on the scepter.

"Are you sure about that? If you hurt me, she'll die."

Lent, huh? If Sasha was harmed, the linking spell would activate and compress the barrier surrounding Misha, crushing her. The knife would pierce deeper into her chest and kill her.

But even if she died, I could simply use Ingall to revive her. Had Sasha not heard about what had happened during the entrance exam? Well, this *was* an era that didn't revive their dead. I guess she wouldn't believe in resurrection magic without seeing it for herself, much less be ready to counter it on the spot.

"You'd better deal with her soon," Sasha pressed. "Even you would need at least ten seconds to destroy the barrier and heal her. That's more than enough time for me."

Sasha's body rose up from the ground, floating into the air with Fless. She withdrew, flying low through the dungeon—

But before she could make her escape, I sprinted towards her, kicking off from the ground. I grabbed her hand in an instant—so fast, her eyes widened in surprise. The linking spell activated.

And Misha? She was perfectly safe. There was no change to the magic barrier.

"What's the meaning of this? Lent definitely triggered..."

Sasha stared at Misha with her Magic Eyes. If she stared deeply into the abyss, she'd see that the barrier, knife, and blood were all fake— mere illusions created by my magic. I'd healed Misha's wound with Ent long ago.

It was simple, really. If the barrier connected to Lent was destroyed, then there was nothing for the linking spell to activate.

"Lynel? No way... When did you...?"

"The moment I saw her, of course. I wouldn't be much of a good guy if I left my friend to die, no?"

As soon as I'd noticed Sasha was plotting something, I had cast Lynel to observe what she'd do.

"Now that I've spent zero point one seconds dealing with that, how ought I use the remaining nine point nine seconds before you escape?"

I fractionally tightened my grip. Sasha grimaced in pain.

"Wait..." a weak voice called from the altar.

I turned without letting go of Sasha, dispelling Lynel as I did so.

Misha got to her feet. "Forgive her..."

Hmm. How very typical of her.

"I'm not opposed to forgiving her," I told Misha, "but it'd be better to have her explain what she's up to first. Such a lame betrayal scene was no better than a monkey performance."

Misha shook her head. "You shouldn't force her."

Dear me. Her eyes were pleading sincerely.

"Please...?"

Fine then. I didn't take orders, but favors were another matter—especially if that favor was for a friend.

"You should be grateful to Misha," I told Sasha, releasing my grip.

She immediately took to the air to run away. "You really are stupid, Misha. Did you think I'd thank you for that? Too bad! Your whole life was made to be used by me. Feel free to regret this until the end!"

A moment later, Sasha lost control of her Fless and crashed heavily to the ground.

"Oww... What in the...?"

"Ah, my bad," I apologized. "You moved so suddenly after I set you free, I disturbed the magic of our surroundings. You'll no longer be able to fly." I smirked at her humiliated expression. "Losers should crawl home on the ground, where they belong. Otherwise I may change my mind."

"Arrogant bastard. I won't forget this..."

I burst into hearty laughter. "That's exactly what I wanted to hear! So you've got it in you after all."

After shooting me a sharp glare, Sasha turned and hobbled away.

I called out after her. "Sasha, I'm lenient towards those who betray me, especially when it's a prank of this level. If you show suitable remorse, I'll forgive you."

Sasha left without looking back.

§ 22. Misha's Secret

"Now, Misha." I turned towards the altar. Misha had already walked up to me. "Will you tell me?"

She stared at me. "About Sasha...?"

"About yourself."

Misha fell silent. "Do you really want to know...?" she asked after a moment.

"Yes, because we're friends."

Misha's gaze dropped slightly.

"Do you not want to say?" I asked.

She shook her head. "I didn't want to tell you."

Didn't, meaning...

"You've changed your mind."

She nodded. "You're my friend. And you're kind."

"I see."

"Yeah..." Misha met my eyes, then stated plainly, "At midnight on my fifteenth birthday, I'm going to disappear."

"Does this have anything to do with Sasha calling you a magic doll?"

If Misha had been created from that kind of magic, it wouldn't be a surprise.

"Magic doll isn't the correct term."

So it was a metaphor.

"Misha Necron doesn't exist."

Ah, I see. So that's what it was. Now I could see the big picture.

"In other words, you were originally a part of Sasha," I concluded.

Misha blinked twice in surprise. "How did you know?"

"Because it's near impossible to break a Zecht without the agreement of both parties. It would be one thing if there were a huge gap in magic power, but you and Sasha are pretty much equal in that area. Despite that, she was able to break the Zecht without penalty."

There was only one possible reason for it.

"The Zecht had to have been broken with the agreement of both parties. If you and Sasha are the same person, that would be easily done. It's just like ripping up a contract you signed yourself."

"You're so smart, Anos..."

My deduction wasn't something worthy of praise, but I guessed there weren't many people in this era who knew of the spell to split one person into two.

"I'm guessing it was a spell like Dielga. A separated source and body eventually revert to their original state."

Misha nodded. "I'm a magically separated alter ego that never existed to begin with. On my fifteenth birthday, I'll return to being Sasha. That's why she calls me her puppet."

So the nickname was because she was living a borrowed life, huh? No wonder Misha wore a white uniform despite having the same power and bloodline. Everyone knew she would soon disappear.

"Was this the work of Ivis Necron?"

Misha blinked in surprise once again. So I was right.

"How did you...?"

"Dielga isn't an easy spell to cast. Only a limited number of people in this era would be capable of doing so. The success rate drops when it's cast after birth, and you two are blood relatives of Ivis—it all made sense once I thought about it."

Besides, he had a motive for doing so.

"In addition to Dielga, he probably cast fusion magic on the two of you. Fusion magic is capable of combining your magic, but the spell is flawed because of its limited duration."

Not even the formula I'd revised could fuse the magic of two sources for eternity.

"However, splitting something into two is a different matter. Ivis came up with the idea of harnessing the power generated when you and Sasha return to being one person in order to eliminate the flaw."

By splitting them with Dielga and amplifying their power with fusion magic, they would acquire several hundred times more power than they should have had. And because they were originally the same person, the flaw of fusion magic couldn't separate them once again.

No matter how I looked at it, it was a reckless move. The formulae involved were complex and the spells were difficult to cast, which exposed Sasha to enormous risk. Would her body be able to endure so much power, or would her mind collapse?

Well, at the end of the day, Ivis was my own personal creation. I'm sure he'd handle it well.

"I can think of several other explanations, but how does that one sound?"

Misha nodded, confirming my initial theory. "Dino Jixes."

"Is that the spell he used on Sasha?"

She nodded once again.

A spell created by combining the formulae for Dielga and fusion magic… He had likely developed it as a way of creating stronger demons. It might even be the reason he'd begun researching fusion magic in the first place.

"And that's why you said we can't meet on your birthday."

Misha nodded. "I'm sorry…"

"What for?"

"For keeping it a secret."

"I don't care about that. Just tell me what you want to, whenever you want to tell me."

Misha dropped her gaze. "I wanted to live normally," she murmured. When I looked at her questioningly, she continued. "My fate was decided from the moment I was born. I'll disappear, and Sasha will remain. I thought I was fine with that. I would live for fifteen years."

Even for a human, that was a ridiculously short life span. For a demon, it was the blink of an eye.

"Because of that, I wanted memories. But no demon would talk to me. As half a Necron, I didn't exist. That continued until I joined the Demon King Academy."

I see. No wonder I'd never seen Misha talk to another demon. Not even Emilia wanted anything to do with her.

"That's what I always thought." Misha's eyes stared directly into mine. "But then you talked to me. You became my friend. You invited me to your home and let me meet your parents."

Misha smiled. She smiled as though she were cradling such mundane memories like they were something precious.

"I experienced a miracle in my lifetime."

It wasn't hard to imagine what the life of a girl who had called my whimsical invitation a miracle had been like. Sure, this era was peaceful. But that didn't mean it was without tragedy.

"Anos," she said. "Thank you for calling my name. I was so happy."

She spoke as though she had to get the words out before tomorrow came. Gently, I placed my hand on her head to dispel the silly notion.

"What's wrong?" she asked.

"Are you sure? Are you truly satisfied?"

Misha nodded. "I have nothing to be afraid of."

She'd said something similar back when we had first met.

"I never existed in the first place."

Good grief. She was such a handful.

"You're here right now—the first friend I've ever recognized. Did you really think I'd let my friend die?"

For a brief moment, Misha's eyes widened, but she soon shook her head. "Not even you can help me, Anos. I never existed to begin with. I'm just returning to my original state. I'm not going to die; I'm just going to disappear. There's no way of reviving me."

Ingall resurrected the dead by restoring the soul—or, if one looked into the abyss, the source at the root of one's magic—that lingered after death. However, Misha's source had originally been Sasha's. If I used Ingall after she disappeared, the source used for her resurrection would no longer exist.

"A body and soul cannot remain split forever."

What should have existed as one had been magically split into two, with a time limit of fifteen years. After those fifteen years, if they did not return to their original state, they wouldn't be able to stay alive.

In the first place, Sasha and Misha's separated state was unnatural. Magic could cause unnatural things to happen temporarily, and it could also restore the unnatural to its natural state. However, magic was unable to maintain an unnatural state forever. If it attempted to do so, it would create a distortion.

"Thank you," Misha said.

"What for?"

"For being kind."

I didn't get it.

"Kind is a nice word, yes. But the word alone won't save you."

Misha shook her head. "I've been saved already. That's why I'll be fine."

What was fine about this?

Just as I thought that, Misha reached up to pat me on the head. "There, there."

Her actions were incomprehensible.

"What are you doing?"

"Comforting you. Because you look sad."

"Sad? Me?"

Misha should have been the sad one, yet she nodded at my question. "Do you regret becoming my friend?" she asked.

"Why ask something like that?"

She thought for a moment, then answered. "Because Misha Necron never existed…"

Her words were detached and lacking in emotion, but she was more concerned for my feelings than her own disappearance.

How stupid. This fool.

I grabbed her slender frame and hugged her with all my might.

"Anos…?"

"There are two things I have never experienced." I hugged her tightly, as though to remind her that she was here, alive in this moment.

"What…?"

"Regret and the impossible."

Trapped in my arms, Misha turned her blank gaze to me.

"I told you—I'm the founder. The Demon King. I will grant your wish."

She thought for a moment, seeming almost confused. "I want to make up with her."

By "her," she had to mean Sasha.

"That's my wish."

Even at this point, that was all she desired. After all, she still didn't believe I was the founder. She had chosen her wish carefully to prevent me from becoming a liar—to prevent me from regretting my promise.

"Is it too hard?" she asked.

"Don't worry. Like I said, nothing's impossible for me." I released Misha and began walking towards the door of the altar room.

"Where are you going?"

"To find Sasha. You wanted to make up, no?"

Misha returned my smile with a faint one of her own. "Yeah…"

"Misha, will you promise me one thing?"

She looked at me.

"Keep believing in tomorrow until the very last moment."

She remained silent.

"You want to live a normal life, right?" I asked.

She nodded. "Okay."

"Good. Then let's go and catch Sasha already."

We turned back down the path from which we'd come.

Misha stared blankly ahead as she walked.

She'd said she wasn't afraid of anything. She'd said it was because she didn't exist. But was that really the truth?

Misha, you may have given up on changing your fate, but just you watch…

…for I am Anos Voldigoad.

§ 23. Round Two

Misha and I climbed the stairs to a higher floor of the dungeon.

"Will we catch up?" Misha asked.

Although I'd prevented Sasha from using Fless to fly, we would never catch up to her by walking at the same pace. There was also the possibility she was running.

"It'll be fine."

I lifted my foot an inch off the floor, then brought it down hard at the top of the staircase. The dungeon began rumbling and shaking. The vibrations were so strong, it was difficult to remain standing.

"Hold on!"

"Okay..." Misha clung to my arm, enduring the tremors. The shaking continued for a minute, then faded.

"You can let go now."

She gently released me. "What did you do?"

"I tweaked the dungeon layout a little. Now we can catch up no matter what."

We proceeded forward. The staircase eventually came to an end, revealing a brightly lit space. It was the room with the natural magic circle that we'd passed through on our way in.

Sasha was there.

She was merely standing there, at a loss for which way to go. The corridor we'd used to get here was nowhere to be found. The layout of the dungeon had changed drastically since I'd stomped my foot, which had turned the room into a dead end.

"Hey, Sasha," I called.

She flinched and whipped around, clutching the scepter tightly against her. "Was this also your doing?"

No doubt she was talking about the lack of exits.

"Who knows? I'm not obliged to answer a traitor."

Sasha's glare grew harsher. She probably had her guard up because she couldn't read my intentions.

"If you want the scepter, you'll have to kill me," she declared.

"We're just here because Misha wants to make up with you."

Sasha's eyes widened. "Are you stupid?" she snapped at Misha. "Did you already forget what I just did to you?"

Her words were sharp, but Misha merely stared back at her.

"I can't believe it. How stupid can someone be? You too, Anos. Stop believing everything she says. Don't you get it? The girl you're so fond of doesn't exist. She doesn't have a life or a source. She's nothing but a defective doll that'll disappear tomorrow!"

"I've already heard all that already. What of it?"

Surprised, Sasha faltered and struggled to respond. "I see... So she told you," she muttered, looking towards Misha. "Aren't you acting a little too lively for a doll? Aren't you scared of disappearing?"

"No. You're wrong."

"About what?"

"My disappearance was decided from the start. I've got nothing to fear," Misha said calmly. "But before then, I want to make up with you. That's all."

Sasha's gaze sharpened.

"I want to know the truth."

"About what?"

In a rare display of hesitation, Misha asked nervously, "Sasha...do you really hate me?"

Sasha didn't answer. Instead, she turned to me. "Say, can we make another wager?"

This woman really didn't know when to quit.

"What kind of wager?"

"I'm going to draw a magic circle. If you can use it to cast the spell in one try, you'll win. If you can't, I'll win."

Performing magic using a circle created by someone else was no mean feat. If you didn't know what magic it was to begin with, you'd have to be able to fully understand the formula at first sight. Normally, the one drawing the circle would have an overwhelming advantage. Unless they were up against me, that is.

"Are you sure? Those terms are rather favorable for me. You can set a handicap."

"It's fine. There's no way you'll be able to do it."

Her confidence was interesting, to say the least.

"What are we betting?" I asked.

"If you win, I'll answer her question."

"And if you win?"

"You'll follow my orders to cast a spell for me."

What a strange condition.

"What kind of spell?"

"Oh? Are you too scared to accept without knowing?"

Hah. She sure was well versed in the art of getting on others' nerves. Instead of asking for something broad like absolute obedience, she had limited her request to a single spell. This would increase the binding potential of Zecht.

Breaking a Zecht would normally incur an extremely high price. Doing things this way proved just how wary she was of my power. The simpler the condition was, the more binding the Zecht would be.

"Fine. I accept."

Sasha smiled smugly and cast Zecht. I checked the contents and signed.

"So? Where's the magic circle?"

"I'm about to draw it."

Sasha turned and walked over to the center of the room. There, she closed her eyes and lifted the scepter in both hands. Particles of magic gathered at her feet and formed the base of a magic circle. This circle expanded until it covered the floor of the entire room.

It was a circle of considerable scale—almost too much for Sasha, if not for the boost in magic power and assistance in circle construction from the scepter and Phoenix Mantle.

Runes began to appear throughout the magic circle, followed by a series of magic gates.

Over ten minutes passed like that. Sasha continued constructing the magic circle, but I still couldn't tell what kind of spell it was.

There were two reasons for that.

The first was that I didn't recognize the magic. It didn't resemble any of the spells that had existed in the Mythical Age. It had either been developed in the last two thousand years or was a product of Sasha's own invention.

The second was that the circle was still far from complete. From what I could see, it was less than ten percent complete. Because of that, there were too many options for me to determine what it was.

"How long will this take?" I prompted.

"Don't worry, I'll have it done by midnight. Before she disappears, that is."

Considering the pace she was working at, she would barely be able to finish before then.

I see. Then this was a plan to waste my time. If I had to cast the spell moments before Misha disappeared, I was more likely to panic and fail.

That was probably her thought process. That, or she had something else up her sleeve.

"What? Getting nervous, are we?"

"If you're going to challenge me, you'd better make sure you're fully prepared. You can use all the petty tricks you can think of, but you'll find your efforts futile in the end."

"That's quite the attitude. Just watch. I'm going to win this one for sure."

Despite my demonstration during the team exam of the difference in our power, Sasha was still full of confidence. There was no way she was still unaware of my strength.

"How interesting. Out of respect for your bravery, I shan't look until the circle is complete," I declared, sitting down and closing my eyes. By casting Tel, I could keep an eye on the time.

Sasha was focused on drawing the circle. The spell was complicated—the slightest mistake, and she wouldn't make it in time. Not that her pride would allow for such a mistake. She drew the spell with immense care and an impressive amount of concentration.

Soon, the sun had set, and moonlight filled the room.

Misha stared at her sister, reluctant to even blink as she burned the sight of Sasha into her memory.

Thus, the hours ticked by, until the Tel read fifteen minutes to midnight.

§ 24. Lie

"Anos," Sasha called.

Finally.

I got unhurriedly to my feet and used my Magic Eyes on the circle, but it was still incomplete.

"Don't tell me you didn't make it in time."

"As if. It's done."

Sasha extended her hand, activating one last component. The moonlight streaming into the room split into countless branches, filling in the missing areas. In its completion, the huge natural magic circle filled the entirety of the room.

I used my Eyes to analyze the spell formula.

The tens of thousands of runes would take a regular caster of this era a whole day to decipher, but I was able to see through them with a single glance. Casting this spell would be child's play. However...

A booming laugh escaped me. "Ha ha ha! I see, I see. You had no intention of winning this match in the first place, did you?"

Sasha smiled. "I know the limits of my power. I'm more than willing to lose this match—but I will not lose to fate!"

Losing to fate, huh?

"As you can see, my objective is to get you to activate this greater magic spell."

"A solid plan. If I am to win, I must activate the spell. But if I refuse, I'll lose, and you'll order me to activate the spell anyway."

As long as our Zecht remained, there was no way out of casting the spell. No matter the outcome of the match, Sasha would achieve her goal. Of course, it wasn't impossible for me to use brute force to get out of it... But that would be distasteful.

"Very well. Out of respect for your wisdom and bravery, I accept my victory."

I held my hand over the circle. By aligning the wavelength of my magic power with Sasha's, I started the activation process.

"I've never seen this spell before. What is it?"

"It's called Zexis. I developed it myself."

From what I had analyzed of the spell formula, the effect of the spell aligned one's magic wavelength with that of another. Unlike the surface-level alignment I'd just performed, this changed the source of the other person completely.

It was a complex spell on par with Jio Graze. Sasha had barely been able to construct the formula alone—casting it was far beyond her ability. That was why she wanted me to do it for her.

The target of Zexis was Sasha herself, and the one she was aligning with was Misha.

"Show me your resolution." I activated Zexis.

Blue particles of light hovered like fireflies, gathering around Sasha's body in the middle of the circle. The light grew brighter and brighter until the room was dyed blue—then disappeared, returning the surrounding area to its previous state.

"Is it over?" Sasha asked.

"Yes, it's my victory. You know what to do next, right?"

She nodded.

"I'm going to use Liknos to ensure your honesty," I said.

Liknos gave the caster the ability to read the thoughts of people within a certain distance. It was possible to block the spell with anti-magic—when the one casting it wasn't me, that is.

"That's fine by me," Sasha agreed.

I gave Misha a questioning look, and she nodded back. With her approval, I activated Liknos.

"Misha," Sasha said, facing her sister in the center of the wide room. Moonlight poured over them like in a scene from a fairy tale. "In another ten minutes or so, you'll disappear."

Misha nodded.

"How's that feel?"

Misha replied in her usual expressionless tone. "I'm not afraid."

"I see." Sasha stared at her little sister. "You wanted to know the truth, right?"

"Yeah…"

"Fine. This is the end, so I'll tell you." Sasha took a deep breath.

When I focused my mind on Liknos, I could hear her thoughts through the magic.

This is the end.

You never existed to begin with. Now it is time to return to our original state.

There's nothing more unpleasant than having a copy of yourself hanging around all the time. Ha. You know…if I actually thought that way, things would've been so much easier.

Back when I had no control of my Magic Eyes…you were the only one who stood by me. The only one to look me in the eye. The only one to smile at me.

Thanks to your company as I practiced, I was able to stop hurting others, just so long as they didn't make eye contact. I was able to go outside and laugh with other demons. But you—you who didn't exist, who only had the company of a servant when absolutely necessary—were always alone.

For fifteen years, I enjoyed my life to the fullest. I'm done. This is enough for me. I'm giving the rest to you.

You say that this is your fate, but I refuse to accept that. Our body and soul were split into two. I'm the original, but I believed there was a way to change that, so I spent all this time researching magic.

Dino Jixes uses the wavelengths of our magic to differentiate between the two of us. By using Zexis, the root of my magic—my source—has become identical to yours. There's no way of telling the original anymore.

It wouldn't have been possible with my power alone, but thanks to Anos, I made it in time. All that's left is to get Delt to work on Dino Jixes, and you'll become the original. I know it'll work.

The final piece to using Delt is for you to recognize yourself...and reject me, Sasha Necron. I've prepared for this moment for a long, long time—prepared to make you hate me.

It's okay. I can do it.

This is the end.

I'm sorry, Misha. I can't tell you the truth. I may have to pay the price of the Zecht, but I'm going to disappear anyway.

"Listen, puppet," she said.
Listen, Misha.
"I have always, always, hated you."
I have always, always, loved you.

Sasha had acted against our contract. In that moment, I broke the Zecht.

"So..."
So...
"...disappear already."
...goodbye, Misha, my beloved little sister.

* * *

Sasha hugged her sister with a smirk, still hiding her true thoughts.

Am I smiling well? I don't know, but she can't see my face like this. I'm going to change it. I'm going to crush the fate where you have to die.

"Delt…"

Take care, Misha. Goodbye.

The moment Sasha finished casting the spell, they were enveloped in a dazzling light. The brightness gradually subsided, and their shadows began to emerge.

Another ten seconds passed, and the light completely faded.

There the two sisters were, unchanged.

With a half-shocked, half-dazed expression, Sasha stared into the face of her little sister. "No…"

I prepared for so long… I did everything I could to put together the perfect plan. There was no way it could fail. Yet somehow…

The murmurs of her heart overflowed.

"Why…?" she muttered, her voice brimming with despair. Sasha's magic had failed. She was on the verge of tears.

"What spell was it?" Misha asked, but Sasha just frowned in frustration.

After staring at her sister for a moment, Misha spoke up again, her voice gentle. "You're a bad liar, Sasha. I don't understand why you need to lie." Her eyes were filled with affection for her sister. "But I love you and your awkward self."

Sasha bit down on her lip, trying to hold back her tears, but one by one, they spilled down her cheeks, unable to be withheld.

If Misha didn't reject her, Delt wouldn't work.

Sasha's plan had indeed been perfect—except for one miscalculation.

Misha loved her more than she had expected. And Sasha loved Misha more than her acting could hide. Alas, the feelings that had prompted Sasha to save her sister had brought about the collapse of her plan.

"Stupid…" a weak voice muttered. "You're so, so stupid. I was so awful to you, and yet…!" Sasha wailed. "I said terrible things to you. I hurt you so much. So why… Why…?!"

Stricken by despair, Sasha fell to her knees and buried her face in her sister's chest.

"Please, Misha, I'm begging you… Hate me. Reject me…" she pleaded, tears spilling down her cheeks. "Otherwise I can't save you… I can't disappear in your place."

Misha placed a gentle hand on her sister's head to comfort her. "There, there," she said softly, wrapping her other arm around Sasha. "Don't worry. I never existed to begin with."

"That doesn't matter! You're here right now, aren't you?! I want to protect you! My precious, beloved little sister—I have to destroy this fate!" Sasha tightly clung to Misha. "Please…don't disappear. Don't leave me…"

Misha gave her a troubled smile. "I won't disappear. I'll just become you. I'll always be with you."

Time was running out. Misha could only remain herself for a few more moments. She smiled happily as she petted the sobbing Sasha.

"We made up," she said, turning to me. "Thanks to you."

"Good."

She nodded.

"Do you have any other wishes?"

Misha shook her head. "I have no more regrets," she said, looking me in the eyes. "I thought we'd never be able to make up. But there have been two miracles in my lifetime."

"Don't be absurd."

Misha looked at me, puzzled.

"The real miracle is yet to come," I said, holding out my hand and activating Gyze.

§ 25. The Founder's Answer

"How long are you going to cry, Sasha? Get up."

Swollen, tear-filled eyes turned slowly at the sound of my order.

"It's too early to give up," I said.

"Can you erase me in Misha's place…?"

"If you're asking whether I have the ability to do so, then yes. Delt, was it? The spell required you to use Misha's rejection as a trigger, but you failed due to lack of experience. If it were me, I wouldn't even need to use Zexis."

Delt altered the formula of the Dino Jixes that had been cast upon them, causing Misha to be ruled as the original body. The use of Zexis to align their sources, the leaving of the final decision to Misha, and the sheer amount of skill and power required were all limiting factors of the spell's success rate.

"You can't," Misha said with a look of protest.

"Don't worry," I reassured her. "I have no intention of doing such a thing."

This time, Sasha protested. "Please, Anos! I'm begging you—erase me! I've lived enough! I want to give the rest of my life to Misha!"

"I didn't exist to begin with. It doesn't make sense for Sasha to sacrifice herself."

Sasha and Misha appealed to me, both claiming they should be the one to disappear to save the other.

Goodness, what an admirable pair. But unfortunately, neither of their contentions aligned with my way of doing things.

"Come to think of it, there was a similar question during the aptitude test," I said, thinking back to the entrance exam. "'Suppose there was a powerful daughter with poor Demon King aptitude and a weak son with excellent Demon King aptitude. A god curses both of them to die, but there is only one Holy Grail to save them. Explain who the founder would choose to save.'" I turned to the two of them. "What is the correct answer?"

"The compatible one," Misha replied.

"Why?"

"No matter how much power a demon has, without aptitude, they can't reincarnate into the Demon King."

I see. Such thinking was typical of this era. For demons that emphasized the value of lineage and aptitude, that probably was the right choice.

"That's wrong."

Misha stared at me. "Would he reincarnate into the one with power?"

She probably thought that picking the former option meant selecting the powerful one to become Demon King. However...

"That's wrong too."

Misha blinked in confusion.

"Power, aptitude—who said any of that matters? Who's asking such a question in the first place? When did the founder ever say he could only save one of them? A god's curse? You think *I* would yield to a mere god?"

I faced the sisters and declared grandly, "The correct answer is to duplicate the Holy Grail and save *both* of them."

They seemed to understand what I was saying. Slowly but surely, Sasha got to her feet.

"I'll save you both," I said.

"But how...?" she asked. "It's clearly impossible. Our bodies and sources were originally one—they can't be kept divided forever. Even if you prepare a new vessel for Misha, we can't survive for long with half a source each. The same goes for reincarnation."

Sasha was listing the logical reasons as to why it'd be impossible, but in spite of her words, she had rose to her feet. If she knew it was impossible, why would she stand?

Sasha still had hope. She was willing to bet on the faintest possibility I'd overthrow such worthless common sense, just like I had in the team exam. I had to live up to that expectation.

"The root of all your problems is the fact you were originally one."

"That's why it's impossible, isn't it...?"

"No. The solution is simple—we'll just make it so that you were originally two instead."

Sasha's eyes widened in surprise. "How's that even possible?"

"By altering the past."

Sasha was speechless. She probably hadn't even thought of changing the past as an option. True magic, however, could transcend time. Of course, when it came to spells of that level, even I couldn't call them easy to cast.

"If it's just fifteen years or so, time can be rewound with Rivide."

"If you change the past, I won't be created," Misha pointed out.

"That's right," Sasha added. "Misha was created using Dino Jixes. If you made us into twins from birth, the Misha here will disappear. Having a little sister isn't the same as having Misha..."

If I changed the past, Misha wouldn't be created. The situation was helpless, impossible to approach from any angle. But the Demon King laughs in the face of the impossible.

"A divided source is fated to return to its whole. But what if there was another source?"

"What do you mean?"

"There simply needs to be two of each of you."

The sisters stared at me blankly, not comprehending my words.

"Let's say a third person was here with us—another copy of Sasha with half a source. This Sasha is also fated to return to her original state. In this case, which one of you would she fuse back with?"

Sasha thought for a moment. "I'm not sure. If we share the same source, either Misha or I could fuse with it."

"That's right. You, Sasha, would have just as much of a chance of fusing with the other Sasha. In doing so, Sasha Necron's source would become whole again."

I gestured to Misha. "Next, let's say we had a fourth person— another Misha. If that Misha fuses with the Misha here, Misha Necron's source would also become whole."

If both sources were one, then there would no longer be a need for either Necron sister to disappear.

"You're not making any sense," Sasha insisted. "Theoretically, that might work if there were copies of both of us, but where would we find those? Are you saying there's a spell that can create an exact copy of someone?"

"Unfortunately, no amount of magic can duplicate a person," I admitted. "Our sources are unique to each of us; only one exists in this world."

"Then it's impossible, isn't it?"

"Guess again. One cannot create an identical copy, but you *can* meet another version of yourself."

"How...?"

"I told you I can rewind time. We'll go back to the past, and I'll fuse your past selves with your present selves."

Sasha and Misha stared at me with uncertainty. It seemed neither understood the concept of time involved in the origin spell, Rivide. That was to be expected, though—even in the Mythical Age, only a handful of demons had been able to alter the past, and just a few mere seconds of it at that.

"In short, I'm going to send your sources fifteen years into the past, where you'll find your newly split source. In both the past and present, your source was originally one. Misha and Sasha are the same person. The past and present Misha are also the same person. When the two sources try to become one, the past Misha's source can be fused with her current source. The same goes for Sasha."

"What would happen then…?"

"Simply put, the two of you will be born as twins, fifteen years ago."

There were countless annoying laws to follow when it came to altering the past. If anyone noticed they were born differently, a paradox would be created and the spell would fail. That's why it had to be performed in such a way that no one would be aware of it—not even the world itself.

"The past will be altered, but both the two of you and Ivis will continue to believe that Misha was created through Dino Jixes. Nothing will change about the lives you've lived; nothing will change in the world's history. The only thing that will change as a result of this spell will be Misha remaining here at midnight."

Sasha looked incredulous. "Can you really do that?"

I nodded firmly. "With your bloodline, you can both use origin magic, right?"

"I can," Sasha replied with a glance at Misha, who nodded.

"There's no reason for me to be in the past, so you two will be the ones using Rivide. You must transport your sources back so that the past Misha and Sasha can be born together."

"Wait," Sasha replied weakly. "I know the fundamentals of origin magic, but there's no way I can cast a spell as big as that…"

"That's why I used Gyze."

Our three sources were magically linked through Gyze, which allowed me to pour my power into them and assist their spellcasting.

"Leave the magic and casting to me. What you two have to do is focus your Magic Eyes on finding your points of origin for Rivide. You seek two of them."

I held up two fingers. "The first is your own origin. Look for when you were still in your mother's womb. This will determine what point in time you will rewind to."

If they could find their precise origin, they would be able to leap back the fifteen years they needed.

"The second origin is the most crucial. In order for the magic to succeed, you must borrow power from the original Demon King."

Origin magic depended on the law that the older an entity was, the greater the power it had. The matter wasn't as simple as the current me lending them my power—they specifically had to borrow from the me of two thousand years ago.

When it came to using origin magic, it was far more effective to borrow the power of the older origin. The magic power would be augmented by two thousand years of time, stabilizing the magic.

But now was not the time to be explaining magical theory. There was just one thing I wanted to say.

"Listen up—I am the founder. The Demon King of Tyranny the two of you believe in is a fake. To successfully use origin magic, you must truly believe that *I* am him, or else Rivide will not activate."

Misha and Sasha exchanged looks. Then, they both turned to me and nodded with determination.

"We believe," Misha said.

"We have no choice but to rely on you," Sasha declared, her voice brimming with resolution. "If there's even the slightest chance of success, I'll happily believe in evil incarnate."

"Remember those words."

I held out my hand and drew the three-dimensional circle for

Rivide. The formula to transcend time assembled around the two of them in the blink of an eye.

I focused my mind on casting the spell, but just then...

With a booming crash, the ceiling caved in. A mountain of rubble came raining down under the pull of gravity, but there was a shadow amidst it that fell much faster.

By the time I spotted the skeleton face, he was already mere centimeters from me. Clenched in his fist was a demon sword as black as the night—an article from the Mythical Age, no doubt. The sinister sword broke effortlessly through my anti-magic, tearing my skin and sinking into my flesh, piercing right through my heart.

Fresh blood splattered everywhere.

"Anos!" Sasha screamed.

"Farewell, formidable demon of unknown origins," muttered a low, familiar voice. Demon Elder Ivis Necron pushed his sword deeper into my chest with the intent of a finishing blow.

"Sasha...!" Misha cried urgently.

"I know!"

Casting Iris, Misha constructed a steel jail around Ivis's body while Sasha called upon all her power to activate her Magic Eyes of Destruction.

"Die!"

All the rubble from the ceiling—along with everything surrounding it—blew away at once.

"Silence."

Ivis waved his hand. Sasha's destructive Eyes were forcibly suppressed, and the steel jail burst into pieces. Gijel was activated, binding the two sisters with chains of magic power.

"You two are important vessels, so behave yourselves. It's almost time—once Dino Jixes is complete, the founder will be reborn here."

Ivis gazed up at the moonlight streaming in from the ceiling.

"Hmm... I see," I said. "So you were trying to use Dino Jixes to create a vessel for the founder to reincarnate into."

Ivis's eyes flickered towards me—and the demon sword still pro-truding from my chest—and he stared at me in shock.

"That cannot be… It's impossible to heal wounds inflicted by the Demon Sword Gadol!"

Indeed, my regeneration magic was barely functioning at the moment, but that was the extent of any hindrance.

"Did you think I would die from a single sword through the heart?" I grabbed Ivis by the face. I had chosen to take his attack in order to draw him near. "I thought you'd be arriving around now, Ivis Necron. You spent a thousand years researching fusion magic and even cast it on your own descendants. No fool would stand by and watch that be defiled."

I drew a magic circle inside his body. The average spell would have no effect on a demon of the Mythical Age, however…

"Unfortunately, I have no time to play with you right now. Leave." I slammed a burst of compressed magic into him and activated the spell. "*Jio Graze.*"

The next moment, the jet-black sun summoned within Ivis tore apart his layers of anti-magic and destroyed his insides. Black light began to filter from his body—then burst.

"Gaaah! Wha— What is this power?! Not only do you have greater knowledge of magic than I, you also possess more power…!" Ivis struggled desperately to suppress the Jio Graze raging inside him.

"Hmm. As expected of a demon of the Mythical Age, you sure are tough."

I tore the Demon Sword Gadol from my heart. "You told me the wounds from this sword cannot be healed, correct?"

I flung the sword at Ivis like a throwing knife. The black blade was drawn towards his skull like lightning to a mountaintop, plunging through his face and pinning him to the wall behind him.

"Gu…agh…"

That should do it. He wasn't dead, but he wouldn't be fighting back anytime soon. I used anti-magic to sever the Gijel chains that bound Sasha and Misha.

"Are you two unharmed?" I asked.

They nodded.

Hmm. There were fifteen seconds until midnight—plenty of time. Of course, the real show was still yet to come.

"Now, time to change the past. Believe in me!" I poured my magic into the awaiting circle and activated the origin spell, Rivide.

§ 26. Keeper of Time

The time indicated by Tel was five seconds to midnight. Sasha and Misha focused on their origins as Rivide invited their sources into the past.

The second hand moved, indicating fifty-six seconds.

In an instant, the world turned white. The floor, the ceiling, the walls—everything.

Another second passed. Then another.

However, the second hand of Tel no longer moved. This place—this space—was now isolated from the world.

"He's here," I observed.

Just then, a tear appeared in the space before us. A silver blade emerged from within, as though someone hidden behind the space were cutting their way through.

The tip of the blade looked like the head of a strange spear, but I knew what its full form really was—a scythe.

"What's that…?" Sasha murmured in surprise.

"I can't see the depths of this power…" Misha added. It was probably her first time meeting someone other than myself whom she couldn't read.

"Stay focused on looking for those origins. The spell isn't complete yet. Besides, this guy isn't an opponent the two of you can handle."

White-gloved hands appeared in the tear, pulling the gap wider open. Once the gap was wide enough, a body slowly emerged. The head was covered in a pure-white hood, and even with Magic Eyes, the face couldn't be seen. Perhaps there was no face at all.

"Hey, Anos...what's that?" Sasha asked again.

"The Keeper of Time, Eugo La Raviaz—the god that protects the order of time."

"G-God...?!" Sasha stammered in shock.

"We're trying to make a major alteration to the past. Of course a god will show up. They can be rather uptight about any disruptions to the natural order."

Eugo La Raviaz turned my way. As soon as he saw me, he spoke.

"*Unforgivable.*"

His stern voice alone was enough to shake the air.

"Oh? This is my first time running into a speaking one."

So even gods could change given two thousand years.

"*Unforgivable,*" Eugo La Raviaz repeated.

"Hmm. It would be greatly appreciated if you could look the other way just this once. We're merely changing the past to save a demon's life. Or is it too much to ask a god to forgive the disappearance of a single tragedy from this world?"

"*Unforgivable.*"

There were supernatural forces at work that prevented the past from being magically altered. Those forces were the Keepers—heavenly embodiments of divine providence, and of the law and order of the world.

The Keeper of Time, Eugo La Raviaz, maintained the order of time by removing factors attempting to alter the past. In other words, he killed anyone who cast Rivide.

"Good grief. Even after two thousand years, you gods are as

narrow-minded as ever. You allow no one other than yourselves to perform miracles, as though you demand a complete monopoly of them."

Ignoring the prayers of humanity, trampling on the pride of demonkind... What worth was there in gods that maintained order, yet brought salvation to no one?

"The unreasonable rules of this world were decided by you gods alone. Unfortunately, I have no intention of obeying them."

"*Disturbing the flow of time is unforgivable. Let the judgment of time fall upon you,*" Eugo La Raviaz said, disappearing with a flash of light.

The next moment, he appeared beside Ivis Necron, who was still pinned to the wall. What was he doing?

"*Ivis Necron of the Seven Demon Elders.*"

Eugo La Raviaz held out his hand, drawing the Demon Sword Gadol from Ivis as though reversing the injury. The blade clattered to the floor. Ivis's crushed face healed before our eyes.

Wounds inflicted by the Demon Sword Gadol couldn't be treated— the Keeper of Time had rewound Ivis's own time to the point before he had been burned by Jio Graze and skewered by the sword.

Ivis was fully healed. No—his wounds had never existed in the first place.

"*The power of the time god has been bestowed upon you. Kill Anos Voldigoad.*"

Eugo La Raviaz transformed into a gleam of light that was absorbed by Ivis's body, vanishing without a trace. All that remained was the god's silver weapon, the Scythe of the Timekeeper.

"Ha ha ha..." a low voice chuckled—it was that of Ivis. "Not even you could have predicted this, Anos Voldigoad." He held the Scythe of the Timekeeper ready in his hands. The sheer power flowing from him was on a completely different level than before.

"The power of a god..." Misha murmured. Her Eyes were as sharp as ever. By looking into his abyss, she could see Eugo La Raviaz's power overflowing from his source.

"The current Eugo La Raviaz erases the perpetrators of disorder using the most efficient method possible—in this case, by bestowing power on the Rivide caster's enemy," Ivis explained.

So Eugo La Raviaz's magic had been added to that of Ivis, huh... But there was something more important to address.

"Ivis, you just said the 'current' Eugo La Raviaz."

Ivis stared at me in silence, showing no reaction to my words.

"That sounds as though you've seen a past Eugo La Raviaz, doesn't it?"

Ivis hadn't seen Rivide before. Obviously, that meant he wouldn't be aware of Eugo La Raviaz's existence either. Even if he had heard about him from another Demon Elder after I'd shown him the spell, those words were still unnatural.

He'd known about it from the beginning, and he'd lied about it. That was the most logical explanation.

"What are you hiding?"

"That's of no interest to you, who's about to die."

Ha! What a joker! Goodness, now wasn't the time to be laughing.

"Ha ha ha! About to die? Don't get so arrogant on borrowed strength. You'll give yourself away." I drew a magic circle before me and used it to cast Jio Graze. The black sun flew towards Ivis like a comet, chased by a trail of light.

However, with one swing of the Scythe of the Timekeeper, the spell was sliced in two. The black fireball was extinguished in an instant.

It hadn't been stopped by anti-magic. Nor had it been negated by another attack spell. He had rewound the time of Jio Graze as if it had never happened.

"No matter the spell you cast, the reversal of time will erase it. Your attacks will not affect me."

"You seem positively giddy, Ivis," I scoffed.

He glared at me.

"Why are you getting so worked up over blocking a single spell? If you intend on winning this battle, you need to at least pretend this much is a breeze for you." I proceeded to draw six more magic circles, firing six Jio Graze at once.

"*Gazelta*."

With a wide swing of his scythe, Ivis cast a magic barrier before him. Gazelta rewound the time of any magic that touched it to a point before the magic had even been cast—removing it from existence entirely. It was effectively invincible in battles against spellcasters. The six bursts of Jio Graze vanished in an instant.

"Bluff all you want. There's no way to break through a barrier that can reverse time."

I snorted in spite of myself.

"What's so funny?"

"I already have."

No sooner had I uttered those words than six more bursts of Jio Graze appeared on the other side of the barrier.

"What?!"

Engulfed by the jet-black suns, his body burned in the flames.

"Gazelta rewinds the time of any spell it touches. A regular Jio Graze will disappear the moment it makes contact, but the opposite would occur if a reversed Jio Graze was prepared in advance. In other words, instead of the Jio Graze disappearing, an ordinary one would appear."

Under normal circumstances, a reversed Jio Graze was completely useless. It acted in reverse, meaning it had absolutely no effect on the world. The magic was as good as nonexistent. But through Gazelta's effect, that reversed time was rewound, and the spell returned to its proper state, causing it to activate as it normally would.

The first six Jio Graze I'd cast were decoys. Behind them, I'd released another six, overlaying Rivide to reverse their time.

"For someone borrowing the power of Eugo La Raviaz, your knowledge of the concepts of time is rather lacking, don't you think?"

A low voice replied from within the black flames. "Indeed. I have underestimated you."

The Jio Graze disappeared. Ivis was unharmed.

"However, with the power of Eugo La Raviaz, I am immortal. You cannot harm me."

Eugo La Raviaz had the power to control time. He could freely manipulate even the time of his own body, so any attempts to harm him would simply be frozen. On the off chance any damage was done, it would immediately be undone.

An eternal, immortal existence. Having gained that power, Ivis was now immortal as well. When facing Eugo La Raviaz, there was one clear target, but…

"I know what you're after. Your goal is this, isn't it?"

Ivis lifted the scythe. Not even my Rivide could manipulate the time of the Keeper of Time, but things would be different with his scythe in my possession. The Scythe of the Timekeeper was the only object that could limit the Keeper's eternity.

"Sadly, I shan't oblige you." He spun the scythe in his hands, then thrust the blade into his own abdomen. "*Je Izem.*"

A three-dimensional magic circle surrounded Ivis's body. His skeletal frame glowed with silver light before his arms transformed into two sharp blades. He had fused with the Scythe of the Timekeeper.

"Now what will you do? I no longer have any weaknesses."

Normal fusion magic had a time limit, but that limit was irrelevant with the power of Eugo La Raviaz. It was now impossible to use the scythe to defeat Ivis. As if that wasn't enough, Je Izem had inflated his magic power tenfold.

"Meanwhile," he continued, "your weakness is in plain sight."

Ivis swung with all his might. A huge, long-ranged magical slash stretched from the sky to the ground, hurtling towards the anti-magic wall I deployed before me. The collision of magic and anti-magic sent fierce sparks flying around us.

His target had been Misha and Sasha behind me.

"Hmm, that's strange," I observed. "Is your precious vessel for reincarnating the founder himself really so disposable? Is it that simple for you to make another, or—"

Ivis gave no response but instead poured more magic into his arms.

"—is there a reason you'd go as far as destroying your vessel to kill me?"

"Do you really have the luxury of chatting? The tables have already turned."

The first layer of my anti-magic wall shattered.

"Impressive. With Gyze activated, you should be under the effect of the King class traits. You've got less than a third of your magic available, and you're both supplying and controlling the power for Rivide simultaneously. Despite this, you were able to withstand my divine strike."

The second layer of the wall creaked under pressure, then shattered.

"Anos…!"

"Ah…!"

Sasha and Misha looked on worriedly.

"How softhearted of you. Your alteration to the past is not yet complete, is it? No matter how skilled the support, origin magic is difficult to control. You'd be better off casting aside those two hindrances."

As Ivis had correctly pointed out, Rivide was still in the process of sending Sasha and Misha's sources fifteen years into the past. There was only one reason the magic wasn't fully complete: they still didn't believe I was the founder. No matter how much they wanted to believe with their heads, if they didn't believe from the bottom of their hearts—from their very sources—the origin spell could not be completed.

"That being said, their removal wouldn't change the outcome."

With a screech, the third anti-magic layer shattered. Only the fourth remained.

"That's enough, Anos!" Sasha yelled. "We'll all be wiped out at this rate. You should…!"

"Run!" Misha called over her.

"Ah, so that's the reason. You can't possibly believe I'm the founder if you have the slightest doubt of my victory."

"This isn't the time to be saying that—"

"Rest assured. I am merely buying time for you to complete the origin spell."

One loud, earsplitting creak later, and the final layer of anti-magic was destroyed.

"A valiant effort, but this is the end."

Ivis swung his scythe into the air. I immediately cast a shield before Misha and Sasha.

"I knew you'd protect those two to the end, Anos Voldigoad!"

The voice that had been at a distance mere moments ago spoke directly into my ear—by accelerating his own time, Ivis was able to approach me in practically zero seconds...and thrust his right arm through my stomach.

"You neglected your own defenses."

The Scythe of the Timekeeper merged with his arm wreaked havoc on the temporal state of my body.

"Vanish in the eternity of time."

Silver light enveloped me, and time accelerated. A billion—ten billion—no, an eternity repeated before me in a single instant. Not even the Demon King's body could last forever. Eventually, it would wither and disappear.

By the time the light exploded, the body that had acquired an eternity of time had vanished—and died.

"Bwa ha ha! Well? What do you have to say now, foolish founder? Fate cannot be altered. This moment was decided from the moment I became immortal—no, from the moment you fled from war two thousand years ago!"

Hmm. So he'd finally revealed his true colors.

"I'm not sure how you've retained your memories after your past was erased, but it seems you haven't forgotten me after all, Ivis."

I placed my hand on his shoulder from behind.

Slowly, Ivis turned in disbelief. "H-How...? You were dead. I'm sure of it..."

Ivis had been born right as the war came to an end. He may have been a demon of the Mythical Age, but he didn't know true magical warfare.

"Did you really think killing me was enough to make me die?"

Ivis activated his Magic Eyes. But there were no tricks to it—I had indeed died just now.

"Don't act so surprised. I merely used Ingall."

"You cast magic...with your source alone?! Without using a single drop of blood..."

Even if the physical body perishes, the source of one's power remains. Those who have mastered magic are able to cast spells with only their source—making feats like reincarnation possible. Resurrection could be performed as long as the magic was cast within three seconds of death.

"However...!" Ivis teleported away, fleeing to a position ten meters behind me.

A magic circle appeared at his feet, from which a silver world expanded. It was a greater magic spell to stop time. The circular boundary continued to stretch, rising over our heads as a dome and freezing the time of anything within it. And not just for a moment—anything within the bubble was trapped in time for eternity.

"Hmm... As expected of magic from the Mythical Age." I stepped freely inside the world where time had stopped.

"What...?!"

"Did you think freezing time was enough to stop me?"

"It can't be! How can you move? How?!" Ivis desperately poured his magic into the spell, but his efforts were futile.

The Eyes of Destruction appeared in my pupils. They could destroy anything in sight—including magic. They were the ultimate form of anti-magic.

"What is this power...? You're still using Gyze. Despite supporting these dead weights, your power far surpasses even that of a god! Impossible. How can such a thing..."

"Do you remember where we are, Ivis?" I asked, walking up to him. "Let me teach you what it means to challenge a Demon King in his own castle."

Black particles of light rushed to where I stood.

The next moment, the number of particles multiplied to fill the room. Countless magic runes inscribed themselves across the walls, floor, and ceiling, and the Demon King Castle revealed its true form. This was the strongest magic item in my possession—a giant three-dimensional magic circle.

§ 27. Demon King

"Come forth, Venuzdonoa."

Countless black particles appeared at my call, gathering at my feet to form the shadow of a sword. Only the shadow existed—there was no body projecting its shape.

When I held out my hand, the shadow rose slowly from the ground. I grabbed it by the hilt. The next moment, the shadow inverted and turned into a dark longsword.

"You said it was fate," I said, lowering the sword. "That with Eugo La Raviaz's power in your body, you have become both eternal and immortal."

Ivis poured every drop of his magic into the silver world, but in that space where time was frozen, I took a step forward with ease.

"I have obtained the power of a god… *I am a god.*"

The overuse of power had brought Eugo La Raviaz's consciousness to the surface of his mind.

"*I am divine providence.* With the power of providence, I am immortal…"

No, this was—a blend of both? Having fused with the Scythe of the Timekeeper, Ivis's mind had begun to meld with that of Eugo La Raviaz.

"*The flow of time is inalterable. The fate determined by the gods is absolute*—that is why fate cannot be overturned."

Ivis's right arm transformed into a huge scythe. An absurd amount of magic power flowed from it.

"*Miracles do not exist. It is all the work of the gods*—two puny demons a mere fifteen years of age would never receive such a blessing," Ivis and Eugo La Raviaz said together.

"Fate? Providence? Miracles? Aha… Aha ha ha ha!" Laughter burst from within me. "Who do you think you're speaking to? Know your place, lower being."

I took a step forward. "Sasha said she would destroy this fate."

Then another. "Misha said two miracles happened in her lifetime."

And then another. "These are the heartfelt words my followers so admirably uttered. I won't simply stand by and watch you ridicule them."

I continued walking slowly towards Ivis.

"*Such folly*—I suppose you still fancy yourself the Demon King, foolish founder? When nobody believes you! You shall rot in solitude!"

The giant scythe swung down at me. The heavy blow tore through time and space—and I caught it with my bare hand.

"What does it mean to be the Demon King?" I asked. "Power? A title? Authority? Status?"

"It's all of that."

"No, it's none at all. Being the Demon King means being myself. And if my subordinates are threatened, I shall retaliate with destruction. It doesn't matter if I'm up against fate or providence—that is what it means to be the Demon King."

I readied the dark longsword and turned to my two followers. They were staring my way, frozen in time. "You don't have to believe me, but Sasha, if you wish for it, I shall destroy your fate. Misha, you said you experienced a miracle, but I can show you a real one."

I would show them—belief or no belief.

"Stop begging. Stop praying. All you have to do is walk behind me. I will crush every conceivable absurdity that stands in your way!" I loudly declared.

Just then, I heard a voice.

"Anos…!"

In the world where time had stopped, Sasha's mouth moved faintly. Her Magic Eyes of Destruction were activated. She was fighting with all her power against the frozen time, and her efforts were extending to Misha.

"Anos…"

They said nothing more. However, the thoughts in their hearts flowed into me through Liknos.

I wanted to change fate.

Sasha's unshakeable will and compassion filled my mind. Countless feelings overflowed from her heart, entering mine.

I wanted to save my sister. I thought I'd lived enough. I told myself I had. But if I said I had no regrets, I'd be lying.

Back then, I still didn't know how it felt to be in love. Dying without my first kiss wasn't a life I wanted to live. But I had no choice. There was no time left.

That was when I met you. You, who stared into my Eyes without anti-magic. You, who had the same Eyes as I.

That was all it took. I fell so easily, it's laughable. But that's okay. You said you'd destroy fate like it was no big deal…but your words back then gave me more courage than anything else.

I gave you my first and final kiss to free myself of any regrets, but…but if I could wish for something, then…if possible…

I want to see where this love will take me.

* * *

Quietly, another voice whispered in my heart.

I was to live for fifteen years.

Misha's peaceful presence and all-encompassing kindness made itself known. Her firm resolution and humble wish flowed from her heart.

I had nothing to fear. I never existed in the first place. But despite that, for some reason, I wanted to make memories.

I wanted friends, but no one spoke to me. No one called my name, for I didn't exist. No one except Anos.

"Misha," he said. Every time he called my name, my chest filled with warmth, as though I was alive. I had so much fun, I almost forgot I didn't exist.

I had no more regrets. I've even experienced two miracles. But…but if a third could possibly happen…

I'd like to receive a birthday present.

"Save me…" Misha said. The girl who'd been ready to disappear spoke loud and clear. "Save me, Anos. I exist!"

Hearing this, Sasha began to cry, tears spilling from her eyes. "Please… Save us, Anos. A fate where only one of us can live is just… It's just too unfair!"

Encouraged by the two voices, I tightened my grip around the sword.

"It's futile. I am eternal. I am indestructible. I am the providence of this world."

"Hmm. In that case, let's see how you fare"—I brushed away the giant scythe and took another step forward, moving within reach of Ivis. Pitch-black darkness rose from the blade, making it look more like a greatsword—"against Venuzdonoa."

The longsword sliced through Ivis with ease, overcoming his layers upon layers of anti-magic.

"*A pointless effort*—this body that governs time is divine providence itself. No matter what you try…"

Ivis's right arm fell to the ground with a flop.

His shocked voice escaped him. "Wh…What…? *The wound…is not healing… I-Impossible… Providence is…crumbling…*"

"What's wrong?" I asked. "I thought you were indestructible. It seems the providence of this world is surprisingly fragile."

I swung the dark longsword again, this time slicing Ivis's left arm from his body, leaving a wound that could not be restored no matter how much time was rewound.

"The absurdity! How can this be? I stop time, and you cut through it. I rewind time, and the wound does not heal?!"

With one more swing, I severed Ivis's legs.

"Impossible… It cannot be! What is that sword?! I've never heard of the founder possessing a demon sword!"

"Of course you wouldn't have—I rarely call upon it. Those who see this blade are annihilated, source and all. Legends cannot be told if there's no one to pass them down."

I pointed the blade at Ivis's throat. "I'll answer you as a gift to take to the afterlife. This is Venuzdonoa, the Abolisher of Reason—the demon sword of the founder, destroyer of anything in existence. Be it providence, fate, or a miracle, all will bow down before me and disappear."

No matter how sturdy, how eternal, or how infinite a thing was, Venuzdonoa could destroy it—even reason itself. Reason was meaningless before the Sword of Devastation.

"You…!" Ivis tried to escape with Fless, but I grabbed him by the face.

"Carve this into your skull alongside your fear, so that you never forget it again. I am the Demon King—Anos Voldigoad."

I thrust Venuzdonoa into his throat.

His source began to disintegrate.

"You... You— *You dare...!*"

In the throes of death, Ivis screamed—in the voice of Ivis and of Eugo La Raviaz.

"You... *You defy providence... You...misfit!*"

The bodies and sources of Ivis and Eugo La Raviaz disappeared. Only the Scythe of the Timekeeper was left behind, clattering to the floor.

§ 28. Birthday

"Hmm. It's my first time obtaining this without breaking it."

I picked up the Scythe of the Timekeeper. True magic items chose their rightful owners, but this scythe and I had never gotten along well—probably because I always broke it while using it to defeat Eugo La Raviaz.

I held out my hand and drew a magic circle. The Scythe of the Time-keeper was sucked into the circle—sent to the treasure vault beneath the castle. It might come in handy one day.

Now... I looked back at the spot where Ivis had been destroyed. So that was it. I knew something had been off about the flow of his magic.

"*Ingall.*"

With a single drop of blood and a verbal incantation, I drew another magic circle. With a flash of light, a skeleton was resurrected. It was Ivis Necron.

Ingall couldn't be used to revive a destroyed source. Thus, there was only one reason Ivis had returned. The Abolisher of Reason, Venuzdonoa, had reduced two sources to nothingness—the two sources that were hostile to me. One of a demon and that of Eugo La Raviaz.

However, another source had been left behind. Before fusing with Eugo La Raviaz, Ivis had been fused with *another* source.

"Rise, follower born of my blood."

After granting him some of my magic, light appeared in the eyes of his skull. Dazed, he stared out at me. Then, Ivis began to speak. "I had long forgotten my master… Even now, I cannot remember him. However, my source recalls this fear. After seeing you fight, I have finally realized the truth."

He got up and kneeled before me. "Forgive me, my most revered Demon King, Anos Voldigoad."

It seemed this was the real Ivis Necron.

"What happened?" I asked.

"I do not know… My memories remain erased. However, I suspect it happened two thousand years ago. After you sacrificed yourself, someone assassinated me and fused their source with my own, hijacking my body…"

So it was no more than conjecture. Well, there was nothing more he could do with his memories completely erased.

"And that someone was to whom I was speaking during the greater magic class?"

Ivis nodded.

By killing Ivis and fusing with his source, someone had been able to act as the Demon Elder this entire time. That someone had known I was the founder and had knowingly tried to kill me.

Both Rivide and Eviy could only affect a predetermined target. During the greater magic class, the memories I had tried to read were those of Ivis. But they had been erased, so naturally, I couldn't. It was impossible to read the memories of whoever had fused with Ivis without knowing their origin.

"I see. So I was shown the incomplete base formula for fusion magic on purpose."

Fusion magic was restricted by its limited duration. If I believed that duration was incredibly short, I was less likely to suspect that Ivis's source had been fused with someone else.

"Have the other Demon Elders had their memories erased like you have?"

"Most likely, yes. It's also possible the culprit is amongst them."

A traitor, huh? It wasn't out of the question. Well, there was no point in speculating.

I touched a finger to Ivis's forehead.

"These are your true memories. Take them. They only cover the brief period of time before I reincarnated, though."

Using Leaks, I transmitted Ivis's memories to him.

"Your orders?"

"Whoever's source was fused with yours was probably an agent of Avos Dilhevia—assuming this Avos Dilhevia actually exists. At any rate, there's no doubt that he who opposes me knows that I am the founder."

I may have gained more information had I spared the demon fused with Ivis, but it was too late now. Eugo La Raviaz's power was too dangerous to underestimate. Sasha and Misha's safety had had to come first.

"Avos Dilhevia must be watching me. Demons from the Mythical Age are a nuisance to deal with—they tend to reincarnate even when killed. I can erase them with the Sword of Devastation if they wander into my castle, but I doubt they'd be foolish enough to do so."

Ivis listened to my words, his head lowered.

"Let's go along with his plan. I'll continue enjoying my school life as I have been until now. If he's planning something, he'll make a move eventually. But if he suspects I've caught on to him, he might turn tail and run. If that happens, who knows how many millennia will pass before he reappears."

Demons had long life spans. That was even truer for those with exceptional magic. Whoever had planned something this elaborate was probably willing to wait forever for the perfect opportunity.

"You died here today. Understood? That should make Avos Dilhevia lower his guard."

If the other side thought Ivis was dead, he'd be able to dig around behind the scenes and find out what they were up to.

"Start by investigating the Seven Demon Elders."

"As you wish," Ivis replied.

Now it was time to finish things.

"*Ingdu*."

As soon as I cast the spell, the white space around us rapidly regained color. The clock hands of Tel spun round and round until they found the correct time to resume from. By defeating Eugo La Raviaz, the world's time could once more move normally.

Ivis had already left and had vanished into thin air.

"Huh…?" a voice mumbled behind me.

I turned back to see Sasha looking up at the ceiling.

"That's not moonlight… It's sunlight…" she said, surprised.

"The space Eugo La Raviaz creates is isolated from the rest of the world. Killing him removes one's ability to return to their original time—but it's only a difference of a few hours at most."

"So it's morning?" Misha asked.

"Yes."

"I thought yesterday would be the end…"

I chuckled. "I told you nothing was impossible."

Misha blinked for a moment. Then, she nodded. "Yeah…"

"Misha!" Sasha jumped at Misha from behind, squeezing her in a tight hug. "Thank goodness," she mumbled awkwardly. "I'm so glad. You know, I… I'm sorry I said I hated you. I love you. I wanted you to live."

"So did I," Misha replied, touching her sister's hand. "I wanted you to live too, Sasha."

"Yeah."

The two linked hands happily, hugging each other, overcome with joy for reaching this day. Misha patted Sasha's head gently as she cried, making her cry even harder. Despite that, the smile never left Sasha's face.

Hmm. What a heartwarming sight.

I watched on patiently until the two sisters readied themselves, nodded to each other, and turned to me.

"U-Um… King…Anos…?"

I burst out laughing at Sasha's meek demeanor.

"Wh-Why are you laughing?! Ah, no, I mean…" Sasha shrank back in shame.

The time-rewinding origin spell had been successful. That was how I had been able to use Ingdu to change their pasts—and why they were still here now. In other words, they had begun to believe in Anos Voldigoad as the founder, as the Demon King of Tyranny of two thousand years ago, and had successfully called upon my former self as an origin.

"Peace isn't so bad, Sasha," I told the confused girl. "A little disrespect won't cost you your life. I reincarnated because I was tired of a war-ravaged world, so this era is pleasant in comparison. This is the kind of world I wanted to create."

That's why I had divided the world into four, and it seemed my plan had worked—other than the odd miscalculation.

"There's no need to act formal. What happened to the energy you had when you kissed me?"

"Wh-What are you talking about…?!" Sasha's cheeks flushed crimson.

"Kiss…?" Misha mumbled beside her.

"N-No! I-It was just a kiss between friends! There was no meaning to it…!"

"Hmm. Really? I was reading your mind through Liknos earlier, and you said you wanted to see where this love—"

"Aaah, aaah, AAAH, AAAAAAH!" Sasha yelled, trying to drown out my words.

I chuckled, failing to stifle my laughter.

"Stop laughing at me, you half-breed! I wasn't in my right mind at the time! I was preparing for my own death, so I just chose whoever was closest! That's all! Got it?!"

Seeing her fluster so quickly from anger was just so funny, I couldn't help myself. Ah, it really was a good era to be in.

"You call the founder a half-breed?"

"I don't care if you're the founder; in this age, you're a half-breed."

I laughed again, amused by her blatant candor. "I hope you continue being yourself."

Sasha turned away with a huff. "I don't need you to tell me that."

"You stay the same as always too, Misha."

Misha nodded. "You're my friend."

"That's right."

Looking over at the Tel face, I realized it was 7:30 a.m.

"Let's head back. If we reach the entrance by nine, we'll get full marks," I said, pointing at the scepter in Sasha's hands.

"I can't believe you," she said. "You're still thinking about our grades in this situation?"

"I've altered the past multiple times before, but I've yet to receive full marks on a dungeon exam."

Sasha's eyes widened, but she quickly got over her shock and giggled. "Then we'd better hurry."

"It's a dead end..." Misha reminded us, pointing at the wall.

"Oh, that's right."

I stomped my foot against the ground. With a loud, rumbling noise, the layout of the room began to change once again. A minute or so later, a path opened where the dead end had been before.

"Would you like to come over after the exam?"

"What for?" Sasha looked at me with suspicion.

"Mom should be waiting with another feast. Besides"—I paused, chuckling—"it's your birthday, isn't it?"

She couldn't help but smile at that. "Then I accept the invitation."

I looked over at Misha, who nodded. "Me too."

With plans set, the three of us headed for the dungeon entrance.

§ Epilogue: Smile

We arrived at the entrance before 9 a.m. and submitted the scepter to Emilia. The academy had to inspect the legitimacy of the item, so she told us she'd hold on to it for a while.

Since the dungeon exam had been scheduled to end at dawn, classes for the rest of the day had been canceled. It was the perfect opportunity to hold a birthday party.

Using Gatom, I transported us before the familiar blacksmith's and appraisal store, Wind of the Sun.

When I opened the door, mom immediately whipped towards us.

"Anos, you're back!"

She ran over with even more vigor than usual, wrapping me in a tight hug. For some reason, there were tears in her eyes.

"I was so worried when you didn't come home!"

"I thought I said it might take until morning."

"Yes, you did, but you're still only one month old! I can't help worrying about you." Mom rubbed her eyes, then put on a smile. "Welcome home, Anos. Welcome home!"

Hmm. Why all the worry over one day away? I'm sure mom had some understanding of my power by now... Oh, how embarrassing.

"It's good to be back," I said.

Mom was all smiles, hugging me to her once more. "Huh?"

At that moment, mom finally noticed Sasha behind me. For some reason, she gasped, as though she'd had a sudden epiphany.

"When you said you might take until morning, did you mean…" Mom trailed off, then turned to me, yelling hysterically. "You meant you were going to do *that* all night?!"

Do…what?

"I did say it might take all night."

"That's not what she means," Sasha muttered.

Wait. Did that mean something different in this era?

"What else could it mean?"

"She means, well, that…you know…" Sasha began fidgeting.

"What?"

She looked at the floor, blushing. "D-Doing it…"

I had no idea what she meant.

On that note, mom ran over to Sasha. "Sasha!"

"Wh-What?"

She hugged Sasha tightly. "Sashaaa!"

"I said what? What is it?" Sasha asked again, shrinking back from mom's intensity.

Mom, meanwhile, patted her head lovingly before asking worriedly, "Are you all right? Was he gentle with you?"

Sasha's face turned to stone. "Um… Just to clear things up, we weren't doing anything he needed to be gentle for," she clarified calmly.

But when mom heard this, her mouth fell open.

"What is it now?" Sasha asked.

"N-No, it's nothing. It's fine, Sasha! Everyone has different preferences. Yup, don't worry. It's okay." Mom nodded as though to persuade herself of her own reasoning.

Sasha couldn't help but ask her to elaborate. "Wait, what? What do you mean by *preferences*? Preferences for what?"

"Oh…"

"It's fine, just say it. What do you mean?"

With no other choice, mom leaned in to whisper in Sasha's ear. "People can have their own tastes. It's fine if you need it a little rough to get you going."

"What?! Are you crazy?!" Sasha yelled, blushing furiously. She held her head in her hands, shaking it in exasperation. "That's why I said you've got it wrong. We were busy all night, but not in that way. See? Misha's here too."

"Whaaaaaat?! All THREE OF YOU were busy all night?!"

There was no stopping mom's momentum.

"W-Were you okay with that, Misha?" she asked in horror.

Misha tilted her head. "With what…?"

Unlike Sasha, she didn't seem to be keeping up with the conversation.

"You know, like… You didn't think it would be better without Sasha there? Or have you come to accept it? You haven't, right…?" mom asked fearfully.

Misha shook her head. "It's better with the three of us."

At that moment, the door to the workshop slammed open. It was dad. And the first words out of his mouth were—

"Anos. You know, your father was a precocious kid as well. I tried to climb the ladder to adulthood before I was ready and ended up tumbling down. Ha ha!"

No one asked, father.

"But you know, I was envious enough when I heard you were dating the two of them at once. And now you're doing things like this together?!" Dad rambled on, placing his hand on my shoulder. "Here's a little advice from your father, who fell from that very ladder, Anos," he said, deadly serious. "Tell me how you did it."

What happened to the advice?

"Say, Misha…how did Anos, you know, jump to the top of the ladder? What did he do to you two?"

That certainly wasn't something to ask your son's classmates.

"He was gentle with us…"

"Anyone can be gentle—" Dad paused in realization, then turned to me as though he were looking at something terrifying. "Anos…are your techniques *that* good…?"

It seemed dad had misunderstood something about the word gentle.

"I said it isn't like that! It's our birthday today, so Anos invited us over!" Sasha objected.

Mom clenched her fists as though she'd made up her mind. "R-Right. It's not for others to tell you if something's fine or not. If you say it's fine, I believe you."

Apparently, the misunderstanding was yet to be cleared up.

"It's all right, mom will always be on your side, Anos. I'll support whatever you want to do."

Dad nodded in agreement. "That's right. If our Anos wants to do it, then it can't be helped. If that's what he wants to do…"

For some reason, he looked rather vexed.

Mom clapped her hands together. "Welp, with that decided, we've got a feast to prepare! It's Sasha and Misha's birthday party, right? I'll have to bake a cake as well!"

Just as mom was about to head to the kitchen, I remembered something.

"Oh, that's right. Misha, there's something I have to give you."

Misha stared at me. "What is it?"

"Hold out your hand."

Misha obeyed, offering me her left hand. "Like this?"

Magic items and their owners were drawn to one another. From what I could see with my Magic Eyes, her ring finger was the best spot for the item. I carefully slid the Lotus Ice Ring in place.

Misha brought her hand to her face to stare at it.

"Happy birthday, Misha. How does it feel to be fifteen?"

She looked at me with her usual expressionless face. Then, slowly, a single teardrop rolled down her cheek, and she replied in a trembling voice. "I was scared."

I figured that was the case. She'd had to endure so much for such a long time.

"There's no more need for that brave face of yours."

"Yeah..."

When she nodded, tears began rolling down her cheeks one after another. Sasha smiled and put an arm around her sister's shoulder. Then—

"I know, Misha. It was scary, wasn't it? You did so well," mom chipped in, despite not knowing anything.

"You know...?" Misha asked her.

"Yup. I was scared until I was proposed to as well. No matter how much you believe in someone, that fear remains until you see your love take shape. And in your case, there's also Sasha to worry about."

Misha's eyes widened.

"But it's all right now. Our Anos always keeps his word. I'm sure he'll make the two of you very happy."

Neither Sasha nor I knew how to respond to misguided words. However—

"Pfft..." Misha giggled. "Both of us?"

"Yup, that's right. Isn't that nice?"

Misha thought for a moment, then smiled again—this time, like a flower blooming.

"Yeah."

It was the sincere smile of a girl who had suppressed all emotions until now.

The End.

Afterword

When it comes to final bosses that seem undefeatable, many characters from light novels, manga, and anime immediately spring to mind. Well, this work was born of the corny idea of making such a final boss the protagonist instead.

I'm a big fan of the sword-and-sorcery fantasy worlds you often see in games, so I took that and added the school life genre I love just as much, then added a demon king—another trope I love—as the main character. Since the story began as a web novel, it was pretty much packed with all my favorite clichés, to the point where it's actually kind of embarrassing to have all my preferences on display like this!

This work was originally posted chapter by chapter on the web, but the most difficult part of publishing a work like that is the inability to revise what was previously written. You may think that unlike printed books, web novels can be easily edited at a later date, but editing the text doesn't revise the content in the readers' minds. Imagine there was a mystery novel that was edited to include a plot banana that definitely wasn't there when you first read it. You'd think, "What the hell? What banana?" right? It's basically like that.

Every chapter of a web novel has to have a small lead-in, development, climax, and resolution for it to be enjoyable. On top of that, each chapter has to connect to the next for the story to make sense.

Once a hint has been dropped, it becomes extremely difficult to edit for the reasons mentioned above, which is why a plot has to be properly outlined from the beginning. This is something I always kept at the forefront of my mind while painstakingly writing each chapter.

Furthermore, some may find this unusual, but the reason each chapter is a titled section is because of the original web novel. I know that many series redo their chapter structures when they're published in book format, but my editor, Yoshioka, kindly suggested we keep things this way as it was easier to read, so we kept the titles as is.

Each title tells what I wanted the chapter to be about, so if you read each title and imagine what each chapter is about, you may be able to have a similar experience to that of reading the web novel.

In the process of being published, I've received assistance from all kinds of people.

First, I'd like to say thank you to Yoshioka, my editor, for reading through the long, long web novel version and offering advice on how to revise it. I've been able to perfect the story even more thanks to you.

I'd then like to thank the illustrator, Shizumayoshinori, for drawing such charming depictions of the world and characters, which far exceeded my imagination. You have my everlasting respect. The illustrations of Anos and company are beyond wonderful. It has truly been an honor to work with you.

Readers of the web novel, thank you for over seven thousand reviews and comments. Thanks to everyone, my dreams have been fulfilled. I can't thank you all enough.

Finally, to the readers of this book, I thank you all from the bottom of my heart.

In regards to volume two onwards, the response to the web novel has been overwhelmingly positive, with many people calling it interesting and the real start of the story. Of course, it won't be exactly the same in published format, but I'd like to think it's even more interesting now. Please look forward to it.

And so, let us meet again someday.

SHU
2 January 2018